"Why am I in a room?"

"They're keeping you overnight for observation."
She tapped her forefinger to her own forehead.
"Concerned about the brain trauma."

"I'm fine."

"So you've said. If the MRI comes back clean, you'll be
good to go. I think it's scheduled for tonight."

Kyle felt bad for keeping her from her life.

"You should go." That didn't come out right, and the
thought of her leaving him alone twisted his gut with
fear. What was wrong with him? Maddie was nothing
more than a paramedic he occasionally ran into at the
hospital.

"Oh, so you're dismissing me?" she said in a strange
tone.

Had he offended her? "I meant you don't have to stay
and babysit me."

"I came with you in the helicopter, so I'm waiting for a
ride." She redirected her attention to her phone.

Good to know that she wasn't hovering at his bedside
because she cared about him, that he'd have to worry
about her developing feelings for a man who had no
interest in love.

Love? He was surely suffering from brain trauma.

An eternal optimist, **Hope White** was born and raised in the Midwest. She and her college sweetheart have been married for thirty years and are blessed with two wonderful sons, two feisty cats and a bossy border collie. When not dreaming up inspirational tales, Hope enjoys hiking, sipping tea with friends and going to the movies. She loves to hear from readers, who can contact her at hopewhiteauthor@gmail.com.

Books by Hope White

Love Inspired Suspense

Echo Mountain

Mountain Rescue
Covert Christmas
Payback
Christmas Undercover
Witness Pursuit
Mountain Ambush

Hidden in Shadows
Witness on the Run
Christmas Haven
Small Town Protector
Safe Harbor

Visit the Author Profile page at Harlequin.com.

MOUNTAIN AMBUSH

HOPE WHITE

HARLEQUIN® LOVE INSPIRED® SUSPENSE

Recycling programs
for this product may
not exist in your area.

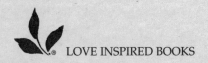 LOVE INSPIRED BOOKS

ISBN-13: 978-0-373-45682-6

Mountain Ambush

Copyright © 2017 by Pat White

www.Harlequin.com

Printed in U.S.A.

When I am afraid, I put my trust in you.
–Psalms 56:3

This book is dedicated to ER doctor Jim Keen,
Fire Chief Chris Tubbs and Deputy Fire Chief Rich Burke
for their help and patience.

ONE

I'm going to die.

The text shot adrenaline through Dr. Kyle Spencer's body. In less than a minute he'd packed his gear and was heading into the mountains.

Can't make it down on my own.

Spence sprinted up the trail, his muscles burning from the strain of carrying the pack across his shoulders. He couldn't think about that now, couldn't be concerned about his own discomfort when Gwen Taylor was stranded in the mountains, cold, immobile and most likely terrified.

He had to get to her.

He'd read desperation in the teenager's eyes when she'd been brought in with a drug overdose a few weeks ago. No matter how hard she'd tried to push people away, Spence's gut told him she wanted help, she didn't like using drugs and alcohol to manage her depression, and the overconsumption had been an accident.

Her last text message had confirmed his suspicions: *I don't want to die.*

He'd given her his cell number in case she had any questions after she'd been released from the hospital. That wasn't his usual practice, but he occasionally felt it necessary. Now he was glad he'd given it to Gwen.

Spence called to speak with her, calm her down, but she didn't answer. Had she taken drugs with her into the mountains, planning to end her life, but changed her mind and had injured herself?

Wiping sweat from his forehead, he inhaled the crisp scent of mountain air and hoped the search-and-rescue team was close behind. He'd left a voice mail for his friend Police Chief Nate Walsh, alerting him to Gwen's situation. He wasn't sure how long it would take Search and Rescue to assemble, but Spence couldn't wait for his team. Gwen could be seriously injured.

An image of his little brother sparked across his mind. His boots slipped on the wet ground and he skidded toward the edge of the trail. Arms flailing, he caught hold of a nearby tree branch and stopped his momentum. He paused and took a calming breath before continuing up the trail.

The memory of his brother's injuries had disrupted Spence's concentration. It had happened twenty years ago, yet felt like yesterday. He resented the distraction. He couldn't let his personal failure affect his ability to save Gwen.

Helping people, saving lives, lessened the guilt about Bobby's death. Maybe if he helped enough patients he'd be able to release the torturous thoughts that kept him up at night. And maybe, God willing, he'd find peace.

God willing? It was simply an expression. Spence didn't believe in a God who could let his brother die at only eight years old.

A gust of wind shoved him against the mountainside but he held his ground, slowing down a bit to ease the resistance. Spence was no good to the team if he ended up needing to be rescued himself.

The sound of a woman's scream echoed across the mountain range. He hesitated.

Listened.

The wind howled back at him.

Had he imagined it?

A second ear-piercing scream sent him into action, running uphill against the blustery wind. Hyper-focused, Spence controlled his breathing for maximum efficiency and side-stepped every rock and tree root popping up on the trail.

He rounded a corner and spotted Gwen flat on her back, motionless. Rushing to her side, he felt for a pulse. It was weak. Blood oozed from her scalp and her skin was cool and pale.

The first sixty minutes after a patient suffered a trauma were critical to her survival. That was why ER doctors called it the golden hour.

I don't want to die.

Spence automatically did his ABCs: airway, breathing and circulation. Her breathing seemed labored, which meant an occluded airway and that intubation would be necessary.

He pulled out his phone to call for help. They'd need a helicopter rescue, no question.

Something smashed against the side of his head and he flew backward, hitting the ground. Spence struggled to make sense of what was happening. Firm hands grabbed his jacket collar and dragged him toward the edge of the trail.

And the steep drop down the mountainside.

Through the haze of a possible concussion, Spence wondered if his attacker was a drug dealer, one of Gwen's troubled *friends*? Had he sold Gwen drugs she may have overused, and the criminal didn't want to get caught and go to jail?

"I don't care what you've done," Spence said. "Just let me take care of Gwen."

The guy pressed what felt like the barrel of a gun against the back of Spence's head.

"You're done taking care of people," the man threatened, and continued dragging him across the hard ground.

Anger seared its way up Spence's chest. This couldn't be his last day on earth. He hadn't saved enough lives, wasn't anywhere close to earning redemption.

Spence fought off his attacker, reaching for the guy's arm.

The man pistol-whipped him. Pain seared through Spence's brain.

The ledge loomed closer...

"Listen to the sound of His glory," a woman's voice echoed.

Momentarily distracted, the assailant loosened his grip.

Spence grabbed his wrist and yanked hard. The attacker lost his balance, stumbled and fell to the ground.

The gun sprang from his hand.

Spence dived on top of him and pulled his arms behind his back, wishing he had something to bind his wrists.

A gasping sound drew his attention to Gwen. Her airway was closing up. Not good. He had to get to her before she stopped breathing altogether.

The attacker swung his fist backward and nailed Spence in the jaw. The guy scrambled out from under him, jumped to his feet and began kicking Spence in the ribs.

Spence rolled, hoping to get to the gun before the attacker did. But his head snapped back and slammed against a rock. More stars sparked across his vision.

A shot rang out.

This was it. The end.

Yet Spence didn't feel the burn of a bullet ripping through his flesh.

He didn't feel much of anything as he stared up at the gray sky.

I'm coming, Bobby. I'm coming...

"Freeze!" Maddie McBride ordered the attacker.

Maddie obviously knew her way around a gun better than this birdbrain who was kicking the stuffing out of Dr. Dreamboat.

As she aimed the weapon at the attacker's back, she heard her father's voice from childhood: *never aim a gun at something you aren't prepared to destroy.*

Well, this might be the day she destroyed another human being. Not something she wanted to do, but she might not have a choice. Her priority was to save the doc and the injured female on the ground.

The guy stood very still for a few seconds, and then kicked the doc again.

"I said freeze, turkey, or the next one's going in your back."

He slowly turned, and she swallowed a ball of fear knotting in her throat. Talk about creepy-looking. The guy wore a black face mask that covered everything but his dark gray eyes. More like black—they looked black as coal.

"Not another step," she said, but even Maddie could see her hands were trembling from the adrenaline rush.

"You wouldn't shoot me." He took a step toward her.

Maddie fired off a round at his feet, coming dangerously close to taking off his big toe in those ridiculous blue sneakers.

He jumped back, his eyes darkening even more.

She didn't have the patience for this, she really didn't. She'd been on a hike, saw the text go out, and decided to stop by and offer medical assistance.

Things got a lot more complicated.

"Down on your knees," she said. "Interlace your hands behind your head."

She calmed her breathing. If he lunged at her, she'd have to shoot him. Time froze in those few seconds.

She thought a smile curled his lips.

Her finger braced against the trigger.

Then he spun around and took off.

"Hey! Get back here!" She fired a shot into the air.

The guy instinctively ducked, and tripped. He hit the ground, rolling…

Over the edge of the trail into the abyss below.

She rushed to the edge and looked down into the lush green forest. There was no sign of him or any movement at all. Great, now they'd have to send a second team to rescue that jerk.

At least he was no longer a threat and she could concentrate on the injured doc and unconscious female. Maddie engaged the safety and shoved the gun into her waistband.

"Hey, Doc, you okay?" She knelt beside him.

He blinked and looked up at her. His eyes were bloodshot and glassy. He struggled to sit up.

"Whoa, whoa, take it easy."

He waved her off and sat up, shaking his head as if to clear the cobwebs. Glancing beyond her he said, "You shot him?"

"Yeah, I shot him," she quipped, then read his worried expression. "Doc, I'm kidding."

He didn't look convinced.

"I fired to get his attention and he fell off the trail." She handed him the gun. "Hang on to this in case he comes back."

His eyes widened as he stared at the gun.

"Or maybe not." She tucked the gun back into her waistband and shucked her backpack.

"You shot at him?" Dr. Spencer was frowning at her. Really? She'd saved his life and he was judging her for discharging the weapon?

"What's the status of the victim?" Shoving his judgment aside, she went to the female lying motionless on the ground. "Hang on, I know this girl." As a paramedic, Maddie and her partner Rocky had rushed this girl to the hospital for a drug overdose a few weeks ago. "This is—"

"Gwen," he offered.

"What have we got, forty, forty-five minutes left?"

She glanced at Dr. Spencer for confirmation. He was looking around as if trying to figure out how he'd ended up out here. Oh boy, maybe it wasn't judgment she'd read in his eyes a moment ago as much as confusion. Could Dr. Dreamboat be suffering from a head injury courtesy of the masked creep?

She clicked on her small flashlight and checked his pupils. The man had the bluest eyes she'd ever seen. "Do you know where you are, Dr. Spencer?"

"Of course I do. I'm fine." He batted her hand away and went to Gwen, as if Maddie's offensive question had snapped him into action.

Good. He was okay. He had to be okay so he could help her treat Gwen.

Dr. Dreamboat, as the ladies in town called him, was not only a skilled doc but he had a charming bedside manner that made young women, old women, pretty much all women line up to date him.

Not Maddie. She wasn't buying Dr. Spencer's smooth charm and overconfidence. No one was that perfect. Besides, Echo Mountain was a temporary stop for the cosmopolitan doc, and she belonged here, with her friends and family.

"You need to keep her head steady," he said.

"Are you sure—?"

"Occluded airway. I don't see a better option."

Maddie was about to offer to take over, but the doctor seemed suddenly confident about doing an intubation in the middle of a national forest with a heavy wind swirling around them. Maddie positioned Gwen's head just right.

"Ready?" he said, making eye contact.

"Are you?" she said.

The doctor ignored her question and used a laryngoscope to hold the tongue aside while inserting the endotracheal tube. Done properly, this would allow air to pass to and from the lungs.

Maddie realized she was holding her breath. It seemed like it was taking forever.

"I think…" His voice trailed off.

Gwen's skin suddenly looked better, pinker, and her chest began to rise and fall.

"Whoa, what happened?" a man said.

Maddie recognized her cousin Aiden's voice behind her but she remained focused on the patient. Although employed as Echo Mountain Resort Manager, Aiden also volunteered for search and rescue. Boy was she glad SAR had officially arrived.

"Spence?" Aiden said.

"Occluded airway. Had to intubate," Dr. Spencer said. "We need…" He hesitated before saying, "A helicopter."

"I'm on it." Aiden called it in.

Maddie studied the doctor. He seemed a little off and not acting like his usual charming self.

"Someone needs to monitor her pulse and…" He glanced at Maddie.

Her breath caught in her throat at the confused look in his eyes.

"Bag her," Maddie offered.

"Yes, bag her," Dr. Spencer said.

SAR volunteer Luke Marshall knelt and monitored Gwen's pulse, while local firefighter Sam Treadwell helped her breathe using the vinyl bag.

"Helicopter is on the way, Doc," Aiden said. "Why does Maddie have a gun in her jeans?"

Dr. Spencer glanced at Maddie as if he wasn't sure.

"A guy in a black ski mask attacked Dr. Spencer," Maddie started, hoping the doc would join in. He didn't, so she continued, not taking her eyes off him. "I got the guy's gun and he ran. Fell off the trail over there." She pointed. "They'll want to send another search team, with police officers."

"Why'd he attack you, Spence?" Aiden asked.

The doctor shot him a confused look. Maddie's skin pricked with goosebumps.

"That's the twelve-thousand-dollar question," Maddie recovered. She felt protective of the doc, probably because she owed him a debt of gratitude for protecting her cousin Cassie last year from mob thugs.

"What are you doing out here?" Aiden asked Maddie.

"I was hiking and saw the text. The guy was crazed, Aiden, beating Dr. Spencer like they were mortal enemies."

Aiden narrowed his eyes at the doctor, who was also a good friend. "Who was he, Spence?"

"I," Dr. Spencer started. "It doesn't matter. We need to focus on getting Gwen to the hospital." He stood and wavered.

Maddie jumped to her feet. She and Aiden caught him as he went down. Kneeling beside the unconscious doctor, she took his pulse.

She glanced up at her cousin. "It's too slow. We need to get him to a hospital!"

TWO

"Bobby!" Spence peered over the edge onto the cliff below. His younger brother's body lay motionless, his eyes closed. Spence had to get to him, but he had to get help.

Spence glanced down the trail. No, he couldn't abandon his brother.

"Help!" Spence shouted. "Somebody help!" His voice echoed back at him.

The wind whistled through the dense forest. He didn't know what to do.

"You know what your most important job is in the whole world? Take care of your baby brother," his mom said on a weekly basis. Bobby was a trouble magnet, everyone knew it. But still...

Spence shifted onto his stomach hoping to climb down to the ledge where his brother had landed. With a solid hold of a tree branch, he lowered his left foot to a knot in the mountain wall.

The branch snapped.

And he fell the remaining ten feet onto his back. The wind knocked from his lungs, he struggled to breathe as he stared up at the pine and cedar trees filling his line of vision. He forced himself to breathe, rolled onto his hands and knees and looked at his brother.

"Bobby?" he gasped.

He hadn't a clue what to do, how to help him. What had

he seen on that medical show Mom always watched? Spence tipped Bobby's head back to keep him from swallowing his tongue. He grabbed his brother's wrist and felt for a pulse.

"Where is it?" he muttered, trying the other wrist.

Panic coiled in his gut.

"Bobby! Wake up!"

"Wake up!"

Spence gasped and opened his eyes, struggling to get his bearings. The lush trees and whistling wind were gone.

His brother…

Was gone.

A ball of pain knotted in his throat.

"Breathe," a woman said.

He blinked, and Maddie McBride's round face framed with rich auburn hair came into focus. She offered an encouraging nod and squeezed his shoulder.

He glanced past her and realized he was in a hospital room, but he wasn't the attending physician. He was the patient.

"You're okay," she said.

There was something in her voice that didn't sound so sure. Her green eyes studied him with concern.

"Who's Bobby?" she asked.

Right, he'd been sucked down into the childhood nightmare. He shook his head and closed his eyes, hoping she'd leave him alone with his shame.

"Are you in pain? Want me to call the nurse?"

"No and absolutely not." His response was more clipped than he'd intended, but he didn't want to be here, didn't want to be a patient.

"Okay then," she said with that same note of sarcasm she'd used in the mountains. "Do you remember how you got here?"

"I…" He shook his head. Had they carried him down?

"What's the last thing you do remember?"

"Some guy assaulted me. Then you—" He opened his eyes. "You shot him?"

"No, I fired off a round to make a point. And—" she paused before continuing "—you're welcome."

He must have looked puzzled.

"For saving your life?" she prompted.

He nodded. It all seemed so unreal.

"How's Gwen?" he asked.

"Much better. Breathing on her own. You did good work out there, especially considering your condition."

"My condition?"

"Yeah, your brain trauma," she said as if it was the obvious answer. "Intubating with a concussion? Gutsy."

She started to slip her hand off his shoulder and he caught it in his own. He wasn't sure why, but the feel of her warm skin eased the panic in his chest. Her bright green eyes widened and her head tipped slightly.

"I... I think..." He struggled for the right words, wanting to thank her for coming along when she did, and for being here to wake him from the torturous dream.

A knowing smile eased across her lips. "How about I get you some water?"

She slipped her hand from beneath his palm and took the plastic pitcher to the sink. He sensed she knew that he struggled to find words, to make sense of the thoughts jumbling around in his brain.

Man, his head hurt. Maybe he *should* call for the nurse. No, the last thing he wanted was for hospital staff to think of him as broken and unable to do his job. He needed to appear strong, even if he felt weak. He wanted respect, not pity from his peers.

"What happened to the man you shot?" he asked.

"Shot at," she corrected, walking back to the bed. "They're still searching for him." She handed him a cup of water. "Chief Walsh said when they find him they'll charge him with assault and question him about what happened to Gwen."

"She texted me, wanting my help, but I assumed she was alone."

Maddie's brow furrowed. "Poor kid. She seemed so lost when we brought her in."

Lost. Exactly how Spence felt right now. Confused, fragile and powerless. Not a feeling he was used to.

"How's the head pain?" she asked.

"About a two."

"Uh-huh." She narrowed her eyes. "I saw what happened, remember?"

"Wait, that sound… You were singing?"

"That sound? Wow, thanks."

"I didn't mean—"

"It's fine, I know I'm no Carrie Underwood. I figured singing would distract the guy long enough for you to get the upper hand. Well-done, by the way."

"Thanks."

"But then, how did he get the advantage?"

He struggled to remember. "Gwen was gasping for air. Guess I got distracted." He sipped his water. "Why am I in a room?"

"They're keeping you overnight for observation." She tapped her forefinger to her own forehead. "Concerned about the brain trauma."

"I'm fine."

"So you've said. If the MRI comes back clean you'll be good to go. I think it's scheduled for tonight."

He felt bad for keeping her from her life.

"You should go." That didn't come out right, and the thought of her leaving him alone twisted his gut into a knot. What was wrong with him? Maddie was nothing more than a paramedic he occasionally ran into at the hospital.

"Oh, so you're dismissing me?" she said, in a strange tone.

Had he offended her? "I meant you don't have to stay and babysit me."

"I came with you in the helicopter so I'm waiting for a ride." She redirected her attention to her phone.

Good to know that she wasn't hovering at his bedside because she cared about him, that he'd have to worry about her developing feelings for a man who had no interest in love.

Love? He was surely suffering from brain trauma.

"Huh," she said, eyeing something on her phone.

"What?"

"A text from my cop brother. They can't find the assailant who attacked you." She sighed. "Terrific, now there's a psycho running around town. Makes me wish I woulda shot him."

"You're kidding," he said, his voice flat.

"Yes, Doctor, I am kidding. Did you ever have a sense of humor or was it beaten out of you in the mountains?"

He was about to shoot back a smart remark when Dr. William Danner breezed into the room. "There he is, the superhero not looking so super." He stopped short and glanced at Maddie. "What are you doing here?"

"I came in the helicopter with him." She crossed her arms over her chest as if daring him to challenge her.

Danner, a few years older than Spence, had a razor-sharp tongue he used to intimidate much of the staff at Echo Mountain Hospital. But not Spence and apparently not Maddie, either. She narrowed her eyes at Danner as if challenging him to pick a fight.

Spence never could understand guys like Danner. Instead of leading with compassion, he ruled with intimidation. The guy was a bully.

"What's my prognosis, Doctor?" Spence said, hoping to divert him from ripping into Maddie. The thought bothered Spence.

Danner redirected his attention to Spence, no doubt a bigger and more interesting target. For some reason Danner considered Spence his competition and would use any means necessary to come out the victor. Yet weren't they after the same thing? Helping patients?

"Besides the head injury, where else were you injured? Ribs?"

"Minor bruising. I'd like to be discharged," Spence said.

"Is that right?"

Spence realized by the slight curl to Danner's lips that he was enjoying being in control of Spence's life a little too much.

"I lost consciousness," Spence said. "It happens after a head injury. I'm fine."

Danner checked Spence's pupils. "Be that as it may, Dr. Carver wants MRI results before you can be released."

"I can always discharge myself."

"You could, which would only prove that your head trauma is clouding your judgment. Is it clouding your judgment, Kyle?"

No one had called him Kyle since his relationship with Andrea had exploded into pieces. He preferred not to be called Kyle because it brought back too many memories. Danner obviously sensed this and used it as a weapon.

"He seems pretty sharp to me," Maddie offered.

Without looking at her, Danner responded. "And who, pray tell, are you to offer a medical opinion?"

"Hey," Spence snapped. "She saved my life out there."

"I didn't realize you two were…" Danner's voice trailed off.

"We're not," Maddie said firmly.

Nurse Heather Warren came into the room. She was in her forties with a round face and warm smile. "I have the medication you ordered, Dr. Danner."

"What medication?" Spence asked.

"Sedative for the MRI," Nurse Heather said.

"I don't need that."

"And I don't need you messing up the imaging department's schedule because you have a claustrophobic melt-down," Danner said.

"Who says I'm claustrophobic?" Spence snapped.

"Hey, what's going on in here?" Dr. Ruth Carver said, entering the room.

Spence was glad to see his friend, the one person Danner wouldn't challenge. Ruth was the hospital administrator who'd hired Spence over a year ago. They had served on medical committees and had become friends over the years, and when there was an opening at Echo Mountain Hospital, she contacted him about joining their team. The timing had been perfect, a few months after his ugly breakup.

Dr. Danner handed Ruth the clipboard. "He's all yours. I have patients who need me." Danner marched out of the room.

"Jerk," Maddie let slip.

Nurse Heather bit back a smile.

"Leave the medication," Ruth said to the nurse.

"Yes, Doctor." Heather did as ordered and left the room.

Ruth looked at Spence. "I'm sorry I couldn't get here sooner. The board president cornered me. How's your pain?"

"About a two."

"At least a six," Maddie offered.

"I said a two," Spence countered.

"But you meant a seven."

"I can speak for myself. I don't need medication and I want to be discharged."

Ruth narrowed her eyes. "You're not acting like yourself, Spence."

Which they both knew was another symptom of brain trauma.

"I'm fine," he said.

"Spence, you live alone out in the country," Ruth said. "If I send you home without MRI results and it's worse than a mild concussion and you lose consciousness, I'd never forgive myself. Please don't fight me on this," she said with pleading brown eyes.

Ruth and her husband, Cal, both in their fifties, had been gracious to Spence when he moved to town, having him over for dinner a number of times and treating him like family.

"Sorry," he said. "I guess I'm proof that doctors make horrible patients."

Relief eased across Ruth's face. "Good, now that that's settled, take the sedative so you can relax for the MRI. It's very mild."

If he was his own patient he'd be following Ruth's protocol without question. He swallowed the pill and sipped water to wash it down.

"They'll be up shortly to take you to imaging." Ruth glanced at Maddie. "Are you staying?"

"Until my ride shows up."

"You mean Rocky?"

"No, my cousin Bree."

"Oh, I thought your boyfriend would pick you up."

"My boyfriend?"

"I assumed you and Rocky were a couple, but kept it quiet because of work policy."

Spence noted Maddie's confused expression. Not guilty for putting her job at risk by dating a fellow employee, but she seemed confused by the question as if the thought of dating Rocky had never crossed her mind.

"Rocky and I are good friends, that's all," Maddie said.

Ruth nodded, but didn't look convinced. "Well, it's nice of you to stay with Spence. I didn't realize you two were friends."

"We're not, but she saved me," Spence said.

"Saved you?" Ruth said.

"Maddie showed up and distracted the guy from throwing me down the mountain."

"Oh dear." Ruth glanced at Maddie. "You are certainly a brave young woman."

Maddie shrugged.

"That must have been terrifying," Ruth said.

"It all happened pretty fast."

Ruth turned to Spence. "Who attacked you?"

"I don't know. He was wearing a mask."

Ruth's pager buzzed and she glanced at it. "I've gotta run. I'll check in later."

"Thanks," Spence said.

Ruth left the room and Spence gazed out the window into the dark night.

It was clear that Maddie was hanging around because she felt sorry for him. After all, Spence had no family, no dutiful wife. Not that the women in town hadn't auditioned for that role many times during the past year. He'd never step into that bottomless pit again.

Never trust a woman with his heart.

If he eventually considered marriage, it would be a partnership of familial obligation, not romantic love. Was there a woman out there who'd be open to such a life? It would be nice to share a home-cooked meal and conversation with someone, and he'd enjoy having a travel buddy, someone who liked to hike as much as he did. His guy friends were great, but they had other commitments—Nate with his job as police chief and new romance with Cassie McBride; and Aiden, who managed a resort and a relationship with his concierge, Nia Sharpe.

Deep down, Spence knew true love was an illusion. His parents had split only a few years after Bobby's death, and his own fiancée's betrayal had nearly destroyed him. Yet there were days when the thought of a solitary life spiked melancholy through his chest.

"Five bucks for your thoughts."

He snapped his attention to Maddie. "What?"

"You were far, far away." She frowned and raised three fingers. "How many fingers do I have up?"

"Knock it off. I'm fine."

"So you keep saying." She slid a long strand of copper-streaked auburn hair behind her ear. "Why do I get the feeling you're not being totally honest with Dr. Carver?"

"You're accusing me of what, exactly?"

"Wanting to get out of here sooner than later. I get it, I do. I was hospitalized for a migraine last year." She shuddered. "The experience made me more compassionate with my patients, that's for sure."

More compassionate? She'd always seemed to have a gentle and consoling way with patients whenever she wheeled them into his ER.

"You need to be straight with Dr. Carver so she can help you. That's what you always tell your patients, right?"

"Sure. Thanks for the advice," Spence said, wanting to shut down this topic of discussion. "You really don't need to hang around."

A flash of hurt sparked in her green eyes. He hadn't meant for that to happen. The concussion was obviously making him irritable. He opened his mouth to apologize, but she spoke first.

"My ride isn't here and I'd rather not hang out in the lobby to be interrogated by fans wanting an update on Dr. Dreamboat." She redirected her attention to her phone.

"Dr. Dreamboat?"

"You know they call you that," she muttered.

"I didn't—"

"Hi, Dr. Spencer." Oscar Burke, a twentysomething orderly pushed a wheelchair into the room. "What are you doing here, Maddie?"

She didn't look up from her phone. "Waiting."

"For what?"

"The ski lift."

"Huh?"

"Never mind. My work is done here." Without making eye contact, she turned and left the room.

He sat up, wanting to call her back and say something, express his thanks again.

Apologize for his rude behavior.

"She's a weird duck," Oscar said.

"Why do you say that?"

"Bossy one minute, friendly the next."

Which actually sounded like Spence tonight thanks to the head injury.

"You ready for your MRI?" Oscar said.

"Yes." Spence got out of bed and shifted his feet onto the floor. When Oscar reached out for the assist, Spence motioned him off. "I'm fine."

Maddie was right. He kept repeating the words, but even Spence knew it wasn't true. He sat in the wheelchair and Oscar adjusted the footrests.

The MRI was one more thing to check off the list. The radiologist wouldn't see anything alarming and Spence would be released in the morning.

As Oscar wheeled him to the elevator, Spence closed his eyes, giving hospital staff the message that he wasn't in the mood to talk. Unfortunately, Oscar couldn't see Spence's face.

"That was some fight you got into on the trail, huh?" Oscar said.

"It was."

"Good thing you shot at the guy and scared him off."

Spence was about to correct him, to say that Maddie had fired the weapon, but didn't want to encourage further conversation. They successfully avoided hospital staff as Oscar wheeled him into the elevator.

Spence sighed with relief. Relief? He was usually outgoing, not the type of person to avoid social interaction.

The elevator doors closed. "Head hurts, huh?" Oscar asked.

"Yes." Spence nodded and rubbed his temples.

"I'm sorry."

"Why? It's not your fault," Spence snapped. "Sorry."

Again, that was not like him. He chalked it up to the hammering in his skull that wouldn't quit. It would make anyone cranky. Perhaps he should ask for a pain reliever to help him sleep tonight.

Then again, sleep would only bring more nightmares, and besides, they were careful not to overmedicate patients suffering from head trauma.

Spence focused on relaxing for the MRI. Being in that enclosed space wasn't the most pleasant experience with the banging, knocking and buzzing sounds filling the tube.

When they got to imaging, Oscar handed Spence off to an MRI tech named Kurt. As Kurt helped him onto the table, Spence could tell the medication was taking effect. He felt relaxed, and even a little light-headed.

"Music choice?" Kurt asked, handing Spence headphones.

Spence stretched out on the table. "Classical."

"Okay. I can hear you so if you have any concerns while the procedure—"

"I won't," Spence said. He wanted this done, over. He wanted to go home to his remote cabin.

As Spence lay still, arms by his sides, the tech slid the table into the tube. A moment later, classical music drifted through the headphones. He'd try to find a peaceful place in his mind, a calm place. He'd always found peace in Echo Mountain National Park surrounded by majestic evergreens, pine and cedar trees—a blanket of green spanning the mountain range.

Green like Maddie's eyes.

That's why she'd been able to calm him down, because her eyes reminded him of the one place he could find comfort.

The hammering sounds of the MRI scan started to interfere with the calming effect of the music. His thoughts drifted to this afternoon's rescue, finding Gwen and the brutal attack. Should he have performed the complicated procedure on her considering his brain trauma? Of course. Gwen was okay now, breathing on her own, Maddie said as much.

Maddie, his defender. She'd saved his life.

The medication caused him to drift deeper…deeper.

He wasn't sure how much time had passed when silence filled the tube. Were they done? Had Spence slept through the forty-five minute procedure?

Heavy metal music blasted through the headphones, sparking a migraine that clawed its way through his skull.

"Ah!" He ripped off the headphones and fought the nausea rolling through his stomach.

The table slid out of the tube.

He was surrounded by darkness.

"Kurt?" he said, his voice weak.

Spence rolled off the table and stumbled across the room. The door, he needed to find the door.

"Kurt!"

"He can't help you," a voice whispered.

Spence whipped around. "Who's there?"

"It's time to pay for your sins."

THREE

Maddie motored down the hall, checking email on her phone. She didn't want to be cornered by female staff members for an update on Dr. Perfect Spencer, nor did she want to perpetuate the story that he'd fired off the warning shot to save Maddie. That bit of untruth had been spreading like the flu ever since they'd arrived at the hospital, but Chief Walsh asked Maddie not to discuss details of the case. So rather than correct the chatterboxes and tell them she had saved Dr. Dreamboat, Maddie had to play the helpless waif.

Anyone who knew Maddie knew she was a determined woman who did not need protecting. But it was too easy for people to assume Dr. Spencer had been the protector since he was the confident and commanding type.

He didn't seem very commanding just now. Fear dulled his normally bright blue eyes. His lost expression, combined with his messed-up hair and bruise on the side of his forehead, made him seem almost…fragile.

Kind of like Maddie after she'd been abandoned. Again.

She shook off the thought. Even a capable man like Dr. Spencer would be rattled after being assaulted by a lunatic in the mountains. Yet Dr. Spencer had been so worried about Gwen that he had managed to ignore his head injury long enough to successfully intubate her.

"Amazing," she whispered to herself. Even if she didn't particularly care for the doc's overconfidence and bravado, she could definitely appreciate his skills. She hoped those skills wouldn't be affected by his head injury.

She stepped outside into the misty rain and paced the hospital's front walkway. Pulling her rain jacket closed in front, she struggled to forget the image of the doctor's expression as he'd gripped her hand resting on his shoulder. As a paramedic, she recognized the expression—fear mixed with vulnerability—because she'd seen it on her patients' faces.

Yet this was different. It was vulnerability, sure, but an edge of confusion dulled his eyes. She'd seen that look on Aunt Margaret's face when Uncle Jack had suddenly died of a heart attack years ago. The same look had pinched Dr. Spencer's forehead when he'd awakened from his nightmare calling out a name: *Bobby.* Maddie suspected Dr. Spencer had lost someone close to him and that emotional wound had yet to heal.

Aunt Margaret said the only thing that kept her going after her husband's death was the support and love of family. Maddie glanced back at the hospital. Dr. Spencer had no family, at least none in Echo Mountain. Instead, he was surrounded by a hospital full of admirers, people who propped him up on a pedestal and adored him. They completely bought into the Dr. Charming act he performed every time he showed up for work.

Would they be able to see past their admiration and realize how scared he was? Would he let them see past his normally affable demeanor into the devastation brewing beneath the surface? Probably not, but Maddie had already been there, heard his cry for Bobby and saw the terrified look in his eyes.

She imagined that was how she looked when Dad had left, then Mom, and then Waylan.

Her cousin Bree pulled up in her SUV. Perfect timing. Maddie needed to snap out of her pensive mood.

Maddie started to reach for the SUV door, then let her hand drop to her side.

Bree rolled down the passenger side window. "Hey, what's up?"

"I'm not sure."

"Are you getting in?"

Something told her to go back inside and check on the doctor, even if he was snappy and asked her to leave again. Being there could help him feel safe, and she owed him that for what he did for Cassie. That's all, there was nothing more to it.

"I'm sorry, but I think I'd better stay," Maddie said.

"Are you sure? I mean, you're here so much as it is," Bree said.

"Yeah, I need to check on somebody."

"You've really got to stop getting emotionally connected to your patients, sweetie. Boundaries, remember?"

"You're right, but this one…" Maddie sighed. "It's Dr. Spencer. I won't be able to sleep unless I know he's okay."

"I heard some guy attacked him. But wait, you don't even like Spence."

"I know, but he helped Nate save Cassie last year and, well, he seems kind of broken."

"Maddie," her cousin said.

"What?"

"When are you gonna stop trying to fix people?"

"It's my job, remember?" Maddie teased.

"That's not what I meant and you know it."

"This is different."

"He's got an entire hospital of people to take care of him."

"They don't know what's really going on. Please don't be upset with me. I'll catch a ride with Rocky when he gets off his extra shift. I just—" She glanced at the hospital, and then back at her cousin. "You always say to follow your instincts."

"It's true."

"Sorry I dragged you out here."

"No need to apologize. Had to pick up something for Mom anyway."

"Give her my love."

"Will do." Bree winked and pulled away.

Maddie felt a smile curl the corner of her lips. She had the best family in the world, even if her parents weren't included on that list.

Maddie reentered the hospital and headed for imaging where they'd taken Dr. Spencer. For some reason she wanted to be there when he finished.

As she stepped into the elevator her phone vibrated and she glanced at a text from Rocky, fellow paramedic and rumored love interest. She was still a bit stunned about that assumption.

You okay? Heard rumors, Rocky wrote.

A-OK. No worries, she responded.

Heard the doc shot some guy.

"Really?" she muttered. Oh, how she wanted to share the truth with her friend, but she would not ignore a direct order from Chief Walsh. He must have his reasons for asking her to remain mute on the subject.

Grapevine's been busy, she responded.

The elevator doors opened to the lower level and she glanced up.

Into a pitch-black hallway.

No lights, no emergency lights, nothing. Yet no alarms had gone off and everything was business as usual upstairs.

She stepped out of the elevator.

A crash echoed down the hall from the imaging room.

Maddie texted Rocky that there was trouble and to send security ASAP. Maybe she was overreacting—she hoped she was overreacting.

"Get away from me!" Dr. Spencer shouted.

Maddie snapped her penlight off her keychain and made her way down the hall. Maybe not such a good idea. She should wait for help to arrive. Surely it wouldn't take security more than a few minutes to—

Another crash, then "Stop!"

She dropped to her knees and crawled toward the imaging area. The desperate tone of the doc's voice drove her forward. As she edged closer, she took slow breaths to calm her racing pulse.

She turned the corner and aimed her penlight into the office.

The technician, Kurt, lay motionless on the floor. She scrambled to his side and felt for a pulse. Strong and steady. He was alive, but completely out. She pried open his eyes. Pupils were dilated. Had he been drugged?

"What do you want?" Dr. Spencer shouted.

A low mumble responded to the question. She glanced at the tech, then at the window into the MRI area. If the attacker was bold enough to drug Kurt, he might do much worse to Dr. Spencer.

She scanned the office for something to use as a weapon. Unfortunately hospitals were not rife with defensive tools. Fine, she'd rely on her self-defense training.

"Let go of me!" Another crash was followed by a slam against the window.

Adrenaline shot through Maddie's body. She shouldered the door open and realized that by doing so, she'd made herself as vulnerable as the doc. She arced the beam of her flashlight across the room.

Suddenly someone shoved her face-first against the wall. She kicked the top of his foot, hard. He released her and took off down the hall, the squeak of his shoes echoing as he ran.

"Yeah, run, you jerk!" The outburst escaped her lips.

"Hey, you! Stop!" a voice called outside from the office.

Security must have arrived. Good, she could focus on the doctor. She took a few deep breaths and turned.

"Dr. Spencer?" she said.

No response.

She aimed her flashlight and spotted him on the floor in the corner.

"No, no, no," she muttered, rushing across the room to him.

When she touched his shoulder, he jerked away as if he'd been stung. "I said don't touch me!"

A shudder ran down her spine. This kind of raw fear looked all wrong on the doc.

"Dr. Spencer, it's me. It's Maddie." She aimed the flashlight at her own face and offered a bright smile. Then she redirected the beam at the doctor. He was curled up, looking away from her.

"It's okay," she said. "You're okay now."

She reached out again and tentatively placed her hand on his shoulder. "Remember me? Maddie McBride?"

The emergency lights clicked on, bathing them in a soft glow.

"Doc?" she prompted.

He slowly turned to look at her. "Maddie? Of course I remember you. How could I ever forget you?"

Whoa, not exactly the response she expected. His eyes looked glassy, and not totally focused.

"Did that man hurt you?" she said.

His eyes widened with fear.

"Don't worry, he's gone." She smiled. "Are you hurt?"

He shook his head that he wasn't, looking at her like he adored her. This wasn't right. The amount of medication he'd been given for the MRI shouldn't have made him this loopy.

"What did he say to you?" she asked.

"Maddie!" a male voice called.

"In here!" She glanced over her shoulder.

Security guard Ted Graves stepped into the room. "Is he okay?"

"Seems to be. Someone needs to examine Kurt. I think he's been drugged."

Ted called it into his radio.

Dr. Spencer squeezed Maddie's hand, still resting on his shoulder. She looked at him.

"You saved me…again," he said. He brought her hand to his lips and kissed it.

Oh yeah, he'd been overmedicated all right. Which meant someone breached the hospital's drug protocol and gave him a higher dose than intended so that he couldn't defend himself.

A man cleared his throat in the doorway. She glanced up at Chief Nate Walsh.

"Everything okay?" he said.

"He doesn't seem to be physically hurt, but I suspect Dr. Spencer was given higher dose of the sedative than was ordered for the MRI. Did you catch the attacker?"

"No, he escaped," Chief Walsh said. "Did you get a good look at him?"

"Lights didn't come on until after he'd left," Maddie said. "We need to get Dr. Spencer back to his room."

"No." Dr. Spencer squeezed Maddie's hand. "I can't stay here. He'll find me."

Maddie glanced at Nate. "What should we do?"

"I'll assign an officer to him 24/7."

Maddie looked at the doctor. "Does that work?"

He nodded, but didn't look so sure.

"If you want, I can stay, too, okay?" she said.

With a sigh, he nodded and closed his eyes.

To say Spence was disappointed when he awoke the next morning just as Maddie was leaving his room was an understatement. He reminded himself that he shouldn't depend on her so much, especially to feel safe. The brain trauma must be causing anxiety, that's all. It's not like he specifically needed Maddie's caring nature to feel grounded. It could be anyone kind enough to offer comforting words.

If that was true, why hadn't he felt grounded when Nurse Bethany came to check on him, or Nurse Tanya?

He felt smothered by the staff and utterly frustrated on so many levels. Dr. Danner seemed to enjoy holding Spence hostage, yet every minute spent at the hospital as a patient made him feel more broken, and more anxious because someone got to him here last night.

He appreciated both Maddie's presence, and the police protection. Without them he wouldn't have slept at all.

Ruth gave him the good news that the intruder hadn't interrupted the MRI, and his scan indicated a mild concussion.

The discharge couldn't come fast enough. Whatever trouble he'd stumbled into out in the mountains seemed to have followed him back to town. What else could explain the attack in the MRI department last night? He didn't want to put staff members in danger by staying in the hospital another minute longer than necessary.

Chief Nate Walsh offered to give Spence a ride. Nate was a good friend and Spence didn't feel he had to watch his words around him, or keep up the charming pretense.

"We're doing everything we can to find the guy," Nate said eyeing Spence in the rearview mirror of his cruiser. "You don't remember anything he said, do you?"

"Not really, no."

Spence racked his brain trying to remember something from the encounter last night. Between the head injury and the overmedication, it was all still foggy.

"Do you remember *anything* from last night?" Nate asked.

"Like what?"

Nate shot him a look through the rearview mirror.

"What?" Spence said, curious.

"Do you remember Maddie finding you?"

In a rush, the scent of coconut rushed through his mind. A memory…

The feel of his lips pressed against her soft skin.

"Oh no," Spence said.

"So you *do* remember?" Nate teased.

"I really kissed her hand?"

"Yep."

"I didn't mean to."

"You sure about that?"

Spence glanced out the window.

"Don't worry, buddy. She knows you were under the influence of a powerful drug. She didn't take it seriously."

Good, because the last person Spence wanted to offend was the woman who'd saved his life. Twice.

As Nate pulled onto Spence's property, he noticed two cars parked out front.

"Who's here?" Spence said.

"Probably locals filling your fridge."

Spence got out of Nate's cruiser and was greeted by Cal, Dr. Carver's husband. "How ya feeling, buddy?" Cal reached out and shook Spence's hand.

"Hanging in there, Cal. What's going on?"

"The McBride clan asked if they could stock the fridge. Since we've got your spare key, I let them in. Hope that's okay."

Nate shook hands with Cal. "That's nice of you, Cal. But I think Spence is a little wiped out to have company."

"No problem. Could you manage five minutes, Spence?" Cal asked. "To say thanks and all that?"

"Of course," Spence said. He didn't want to seem ungrateful, or rude.

Acting unusually curt would cause Drs. Carver and Danner to question the severity of his brain injury. Although his injury didn't look serious on the scan, brain injuries were all different and unpredictable. TBI victims could experience mood swings, or personality changes, which was what his doctors would be looking for.

Spence had always worn a smile as his armor, but today his head hurt and his body ached. He wanted to relax without having to smile or make pleasant conversation.

"Your assistant is supposed to start tonight," Cal said.

"Assistant?" Spence questioned.

"Ruth hired someone to help you out until you're fully recovered," Cal said.

"That's not necessary."

"Perhaps not, but she doesn't want to take any chances. She found someone to check in on you for the next week or so, until you're up and running at your usual 120 percent."

Spence suspected it might take longer than a week. Two or three perhaps? What if he never cleared the clutter from his brain, and had to give up practicing medicine? He fisted his hand, frustrated at the thought of not being a doctor, not saving lives.

His life would be, in a word, over. Panic overwhelmed him.

Get it together, Spence. He pulled himself back from the edge. He'd be okay; he had to be okay. He was just exhausted.

The men went to the cabin and Cal swung open the door.

Margaret, matriarch of the McBride clan, was directing her daughter, Cassie, on building a fire.

Cassie glanced over her shoulder, dropped the kindling and ran into Nate's arms. "Hi, Chief. I could use your fire expertise."

Spence noticed Nate's face light up as he hugged his girlfriend.

"With pleasure, dear," he said, teasingly.

"Dr. Spencer, it's so good to see you up and around," Margaret said.

"Thank you."

A light, melodic sound echoed from the kitchen. Spence glanced across the cabin. Maddie stood at the counter with her back to the group, singing along with a song playing through her earbuds.

"And I always knew…with your love…"

"Maddie?" her aunt Margaret said.

"I could do anything…"

"Maddie!" her aunt tried again.

Cassie grabbed a piece of kindling and tossed it at her cousin to get her attention.

Maddie shrieked and spun around, wielding a chopping knife like a weapon. She glanced at the utensil in her hand and scrunched her nose. Removing the earbuds, she offered a smile, blushing. "Sorry. Got lost in the music. Hi, Doc. Hi, Chief."

"Maddie, nice to see you," Nate said.

"I didn't know there'd be four for dinner." Maddie glanced over her shoulder at the vegetables she'd been chopping.

"Actually, I've got an appointment," Cal said.

"I won't be staying for dinner, either," Nate said.

"Hey, my cooking isn't that bad," Maddie joked.

Joked. Smiled. Cooked. Spence enjoyed the moment, however fleeting.

"It's not your cooking, coz," Cassie said. "Chief promised me dinner at Mackey's Dim Sum tonight."

"Nice," Maddie said with envy in her voice.

Spence suddenly wanted to take Maddie out to dinner.

Okay, now he was really losing his mind.

"Well, I'm off," Cal said.

"Could I have the spare key for the officer who will be keeping watch?" Nate asked.

"Sure, Chief. Spence, your assistant should be checking in at eight. Well, have a good night, everyone." Cal handed Nate the key and left.

"Your assistant?" Maddie asked.

"Dr. Carver hired someone to keep an eye on me," Spence explained.

"Ah," Maddie said, and went back to chopping vegetables.

Something felt off, Spence wasn't sure what. He and Maddie hadn't spoken about what had happened in the MRI room, and they probably should. At the very least he should apologize for kissing her hand.

"I brewed some herbal tea from Healthy Eats," Maddie

said. "It's especially good for healing. Would you like a cup, Dr. Spencer?"

"Maddie, you're in my home, making me dinner. Call me Spence like everyone else."

"Yes, sir."

"And no sir stuff."

"Okay, Spence."

It sounded strange coming out of her mouth, unusually intimate. Nate helped his girlfriend build the fire, and Margaret assisted Maddie with dinner preparation.

"So tea, yes?" Maddie asked.

"Yes, thank you." Spence wandered to the living room sofa and collapsed.

"We'll be out of your hair in a few minutes, Doctor," Margaret said.

"Thanks."

The cabin had an open floor plan along with two private bedrooms, so Maddie was never out of Spence's sight. For some reason he liked being able to watch her auburn ponytail dance across her shoulders as she moved back and forth from the refrigerator to the sink.

This had to stop. He ripped his gaze from Maddie in time to see Nate kiss Cassie on the cheek.

"I'll pick you up at seven," Nate said.

"I'll be ready." When Cassie hugged him, Spence had to look away.

The love shared between those two was palpable. Spence had accepted the fact he wasn't meant to experience romantic love, but some days he ached for what he was missing. No, it was the head injury messing with him, making him moody, that's all.

"Come on, Ma." Cassie motioned to Margaret.

"But I'm not done helping—"

"I can finish," Maddie said. "I think the chief has to ask me some questions anyway, so I'll stick around a little while."

Margaret grabbed her purse and smiled at Spence. "You're in our prayers, Doctor."

"Thank you, Margaret," he said.

"Don't be late," Cassie said to Nate.

"Am I ever?"

"That means no police emergencies, either." Cassie winked and shut the door behind her and her mom.

"If only that were up to me," Nate said softly. He joined Spence in the living room, sitting on the sofa. "How ya feeling, buddy?"

"Better, now that I'm home."

Nate glanced across the cabin. "Maddie, can you take a break? You should hear this, too."

Spence didn't like the sound of that. He didn't want Maddie to be threatened by the danger stalking him.

When Maddie joined them, Spence noticed a few strands of hair had escaped her ponytail, framing her face. He snapped his attention from her and looked at Nate.

"We went through video footage from the hospital and came up with this." Nate flashed a photo on his phone of a man in a black jacket with a cap pulled low over his forehead.

"It's the same guy from the mountains," Maddie said.

"How can you be sure? You can't see his face," Nate said.

"His shoes squeaked. I heard it in the mountains, and again after he shoved me against the wall and ran out of the MRI room."

It felt like someone punched Spence in the gut. "He shoved you against the wall?"

"I'm fine, and he is too apparently. Obviously survived the fall off the trail. Do you have any better images?"

"Unfortunately not." Nate pocketed his phone. "He disappeared right in front of security."

"How is that possible?" Spence asked, growing more frustrated.

"We're not sure," Nate said.

"What about Kurt? Did he remember anything?" Maddie asked.

"Nothing usable," Nate said. "The attacker got him by the throat and stuck him with a syringe. As he was losing consciousness he said he saw a gorilla."

"Whoa, that was some drug," Maddie said.

"What we can't figure out is why he came after you at the hospital, Spence," Nate said. "At first this looked like you randomly stepped into trouble when you went to help Gwen. Now I'm not so sure that's all it is. I hate to ask, but can you think of anyone who'd want to hurt you?"

"Hurt me?" Spence scoffed. "Dr. Dreamboat?"

Nate and Maddie weren't smiling.

"What?" Spence challenged, anxiety trickling across his nerve endings.

"You're being awfully cavalier about this," Nate said.

"As opposed to what, launching into full-blown panic?" Which was exactly where he was going. Then he remembered the emails.

"What is it?" Nate said, eyeing him.

"Nothing."

"It's something if it made you frown like that," Maddie said.

"I started getting emails about a month ago. Nasty emails."

"Nasty, as in threatening?" Nate pushed.

"You could say that, but anyone can send an email. That doesn't mean they'd concoct a plan to come after me."

"We'll need to look at those emails," Nate said. "In the meantime I've assigned an off-duty officer on the cabin until we find the assailant."

Frustration bubbled up in Spence's chest. "Yeah, right. We don't even know what he looks like." Spence stood. "I need an aspirin."

"I can get it."

"No," he snapped at Maddie. "You need to leave."

"Spence?" Nate questioned his friend's abruptness.

"Look, if you're right and I'm in danger then I don't want Maddie anywhere near me."

"But—"

"Thanks for making dinner, Maddie," he interrupted her. "Please let yourself out." Spence marched into his bedroom and shut the door, feeling like a total jerk, but he truly didn't want to put Maddie at risk.

Besides, he craved peace and quiet to calm the annoying anxiety taunting him. He struggled to accept the fact that he could be a killer's primary target. He'd tried joking it off because the thought of someone coming for him in his current, damaged state was more than he could process.

His head ached and his world seemed to be teetering on rocky ground. All he wanted was time alone to regroup. Instead Maddie was here offering to get him aspirin; cooking him dinner.

Blinking those adorable green eyes at him.

Singing heartfelt songs about love.

He stumbled toward the bed and flopped down on his stomach. It was rude to walk out on Nate and Maddie like that, but he didn't have another ounce of energy to continue the conversation. Hopefully she'd pack up her things and leave.

Go home.

Where she'd be safe.

An hour later Maddie had finished the food prep, done the dishes and set the table for Dr. Spencer's dinner. There were no more excuses to hang around.

He'd given her a firm order to leave, which meant technically she was trespassing.

Something niggled at her brain as she headed for the door. Hesitating, she glanced at his bedroom door, wondering if she should check on him before she left. His assistant wasn't going to be here for another hour.

A soft knock echoed from the front door. She cracked it open and greeted off-duty police officer Red Carrington.

"Hi, Red."

"Maddie. The chief wanted me to make sure you were okay in here."

"The chief should be focused on his date."

Red frowned in confusion.

"He's out with my cousin Cassie."

"Ah, right. How's the doc?" Red glanced over her shoulder into the cabin.

"I was actually going to check on him before I left. Did you want some coffee or dinner? There's plenty of food."

"Nah, I brought a sandwich from home. I've got the key to the cabin to lock up after you leave."

"Great, thanks. Just give me a few minutes."

"Take your time."

She shut and locked the front door, grateful to Nate for assigning an officer to Dr. Spencer's cabin. No matter how aloof he seemed, the doc knew he was in trouble and it had to terrify him, especially in his current state.

Heading for his room, she decided she'd take his pulse and check him for a fever, not that she expected him to have one. If he seemed okay, she could leave with a clear mind and calm heart. She wouldn't be up all night worrying about him.

Really, Maddie? She wondered how she'd become so attached to the doc and figured it was twofold: she could never repay him for saving her cousin Cassie's life, plus, Maddie was a fixer at her core. If she saw someone in emotional turmoil, she did everything within her power to help ease his pain.

Whether he wanted to admit it or not, Dr. Spencer was certainly in trouble.

She turned the doorknob to his bedroom, relieved that it wasn't locked. "Dr. Spencer?"

The room was dark except for the shaft of light streaming

in from the living room behind her. The doc was stretched diagonally across the bed on his stomach.

She considered her options. She didn't want to turn on the light and rouse him from much-needed sleep. He got little sleep last night in the hospital thanks to nightmares that plagued him until about 3:00 a.m. It was a good thing she'd stayed to awaken him from the terror each time he'd called out the name *Bobby.*

Maddie went to his bedside, knelt and took his pulse. Solid at sixty beats per minute. She placed her palm across his forehead. It was cool to the touch, not warm and clammy. Still, should she wake him to check his pupils?

No, if Dr. Carver suspected it was more serious than a mild concussion she wouldn't have discharged him. Maddie pulled the comforter across the bed to cover his body. He looked so peaceful. She sighed, glad he wasn't thrashing about, tortured by nightmares.

Since there was nothing more she could do for him, she decided to scoot. If Spence awakened and found her hovering, he'd surely be cross. She'd leave the doctor in the capable hands of Officer Carrington.

As she made her way to the front door, she considered taking a personal day off work tomorrow. She had plenty coming, actually enough days to piece together a nice trip somewhere. A vacation would be perfect right about now, especially after the craziness of the last twenty-four hours.

She opened the front door and froze.

The driver's side door of Officer Carrington's car was open but he was nowhere in sight.

"Red?" she called out.

A gunshot echoed across the property.

FOUR

Maddie darted inside the cabin and slammed the door, her heart hammering against her chest. Was it the masked man from the mountains? Had he tracked Dr. Spencer home, waiting for the best moment to attack?

Officer Carrington must have seen the guy stalking the cabin and went after him.

She hoped. She prayed. She also prayed that Red had been the one to fire the shot, perhaps a warning shot, to get the guy to stop. Yeah, she knew how well that did *not* work when she'd fired a warning shot. On the off chance the masked attacker neutralized the police officer, she had to focus on protecting herself and the doctor.

Since his curtainless living room windows exposed them to the world, she clicked off all the lights. Snapping the small flashlight off her keychain, she aimed the beam and made her way into the bedroom.

She pulled her phone out of her pocket and called emergency.

"9-1-1, what's your emergency?"

"This is Maddie McBride. I'm at Dr. Kyle Spencer's cabin and I heard gunfire outside."

"We have an officer posted on the premises."

"He's not in his car. Send help, and notify Chief Walsh ASAP."

Someone pounded on the front door, obviously not Red because he had a key to the cabin.

"He's trying to get in," she said to the operator. "I have to go."

"Maddie, please stay on the line."

Shoving the phone into her pocket, she crouched beside Dr. Spencer. She could only focus on one thing at a time, and right now her priority was to keep herself and Spence alive.

She clicked on his nightstand lamp. Shades covered his windows, probably so he could sleep after getting off a night shift at the hospital.

"Spence, wake up." She gave his shoulder a gentle nudge.

More pounding echoed from the front door.

"Spence?" When that didn't work, she decided to use his full name. "Dr. Kyle Spencer, wake up."

The doctor moaned and blinked his eyes open. "What, where am I?"

Her breath caught in her throat. Did he really not know he was in his own bedroom? Or was he disoriented because she'd awakened him from a deep sleep?

"What is that racket?" He rolled onto his back and threw an arm across his eyes as if he intended to fall back asleep.

"You can't go back to sleep. Someone's trying to break in."

"What?" He sat up abruptly and gripped his head with both hands. "Ah, man." He looked at her with bloodshot eyes. "What are you still doing here?"

"Yell at me later. Do you keep any weapons in the cabin?"

"I'm a doctor," he said, as if that was explanation enough.

"So no weapons then."

"Is it the same guy?"

"Unless you have other enemies we don't know about."

He shot her a look, then said, "We can sneak out through the window." He wavered as he crossed the room, looking like someone who'd been overserved at the local pub.

Maddie knew that running wasn't an option. With Spence

in his current state they'd be easy prey in the wilderness. At least inside the cabin they could hold their ground.

His started to open the window.

"Don't," she said. "I've got a better idea. I saw chili powder in your kitchen earlier."

"Chili powder?"

"Come on." She motioned to him.

Instead, he stared at her.

The pounding stopped. Which was not necessarily a good thing. The guy could be gearing up to bust his way through the door with an ax. She'd noticed one on the front porch, probably for chopping wood.

She dashed out of the bedroom and whipped open a kitchen cabinet. Spence came up behind her, opened a drawer and took out a butcher knife. He glanced at her, the knife clutched in his hand.

"He could just as easily use that on us." She grabbed chili powder and flung open the cabinet beneath the sink. "Here, you take the fire extinguisher." She handed it to him. "Spray him in the face and whack him over the head with the tank. Got it?"

"Spray and whack, sure."

There wasn't much confidence in his voice. He was probably still groggy from sleep, or the head injury, or a combination of both.

She'd have to rely on her own strength and determination to get them out of this dangerous situation.

Tapping echoed from the bedroom. The guy was trying to get in through the bedroom window. She encouraged the doctor to crouch behind the kitchen island, out of sight. "Stay down."

She spotted a hiking stick propped against the wall by the front door. After temporarily blinding the attacker with the chili powder, she'd use the stick as a defensive weapon. Karate class would come in handy tonight.

She would position herself behind a large leather armchair, the perfect position from which to make her attack. On her way to the hiding spot, she opened the front door to confuse the intruder, making it look like she and the doc had fled—a risky move if there was a second assailant but good strategy if the guy was alone.

She'd be ready either way.

A crash echoed from the bedroom.

Heart hammering against her chest, she ducked behind the chair, gripping the stick in one hand and the chili powder in the other. No one entered through the front door, which was certainly a good sign. It meant they were dealing with only the one intruder who had breached the bedroom window, most likely the same guy who'd attacked the doctor in the mountains and shoved her against the wall in the hospital last night.

Maddie waited, calmed her breathing and prayed to God for help. She wasn't a violent person by nature, but needed to do what was necessary to protect herself and the doc.

The wooden floorboards creaked as the guy made his way through the cabin.

"Doctor?" he said. "Where are you?"

Silence rang in her ears.

"Get out of my cabin!" Dr. Spencer ordered.

What? She'd told him to stay hidden, out of sight. Did his brain injury cause him to forget her instructions? Maddie peered around the chair she was using as cover. The intruder was stalking Dr. Spencer from the other side of the kitchen island.

"You need to come with me," the guy said.

"Why, so you can kill me?" Spence was gripping the fire extinguisher to his chest, but not pointing it at the guy.

The guy was tall, broad-shouldered, wearing a black jacket but no mask, which meant he wasn't worried about being identified because he planned to kill the witness to this attack.

He planned to kill the doctor.

But Spence wasn't the only witness.

The assailant drew a knife. "One way or another, Doc."

Maddie jumped out of her hiding spot. "Hey!"

The guy turned to her, more irritated than anything else. He had a full beard of dark hair and piercing brown eyes.

He started toward her.

"The cops are on the way," she said, clutching the hiking stick.

She had to make him drop the knife.

He took a step closer. "You weren't supposed to be here."

If only he'd get close enough. She fingered the container of chili powder in her other hand.

Spence suddenly grabbed him from behind.

"No!" she cried, fearing the bearded guy would slash him with the knife.

The guy elbowed Spence in the ribs and the doctor released his grip, dropping to his knees.

As the stranger turned his attention to Maddie, she lunged…

Hurling chili powder into his eyes.

The guy cried out and made a wide arc with the knife. Gripping the walking stick with both hands, she nailed him in the gut. He pitched forward, faltering as he tried to get away from her.

She smacked him again, and again.

Flailing his arms, he couldn't see her well enough to hit his mark. She had no problem hitting hers.

"Out of here!" she shouted, delivering firm strikes to his ribs, arms and shoulders, forcing him backward. He stumbled out the open front door. She slammed it shut and flipped the dead bolt.

She rushed to Spence's side. "Are you—?"

"Fine," he said.

"Come on." She grabbed his arm and led him into the bedroom. "We need to block the window!"

She didn't think the intruder would try another attack,

not with blurred vision from the chili powder and bruised ribs, but she couldn't be sure. Spence helped her shoulder an armoire in front of the now glassless window.

Shutting the bedroom door, she scanned the room, grabbed a chair and wedged it against the handle. Even if the intruder got in through a living room window, he wasn't getting into the bedroom.

Backing up against the empty wall where the armoire had been, she took a deep breath and reminded herself it wasn't over until the police arrived.

She had to be ready for whatever happened next.

Spence shifted onto the edge of the bed. Silence stretched between them, the sound of her heart pounding against her eardrums.

"You're a ninja," Dr. Spencer said.

She glanced at him. "What?"

"The way you used my hiking stick as a weapon. You're a ninja."

"And you're an idiot," she let slip.

He looked up at her with a confused expression.

"I told you to stay hidden, but you jumped up like a jack-in-the-box and announced yourself. What was that about?"

"I was trying to distract him, so he wouldn't hurt you."

Maddie was speechless. Even in his injured state, Dr. Spencer was trying to protect her?

"I had a hard time figuring out how to activate the extinguisher, sorry," he said.

"We should keep quiet and listen."

"I doubt he'll come back. You gave him at least three broken ribs by my count."

She didn't respond, trying to stay in the present, and not relive what had just happened. With full concentration on the now, she could effectively catalog every sound that tweaked her eardrums.

"Thanks for saving my life," he said, "again."

She didn't want his thanks. She wanted him to get better so he could defend himself. She wanted him to use his common sense. He was in no condition to protect Maddie from harm. It was pretty obvious she didn't need his help, or anyone else's for that matter.

"Where'd you learn that stuff with the stick?" Spence asked.

"Martial arts class."

"Guess I should sign up."

"How can you be so aloof?" she said.

"Not sure how the alternative would help."

He was right, although Maddie still couldn't calm her racing pulse. Her phone vibrated and she answered with one hand, while gripping the stick with her other. "Hello?"

"It's Nate."

"The guy broke in. We forced him out, but he might still be on the premises."

"Officer Carrington called in suspicious activity and went silent."

"I heard a gunshot. I haven't seen him since then."

"I'm en route, along with another cruiser. Two minutes tops."

"Thanks."

The fact that help was close eased the tension in her shoulders. Taking a deep breath, she said a prayer of thanks for giving her the strength to snap into action so quickly.

"What's wrong?" Spence said.

"Why do you think something's wrong?"

"You're humming."

"I am?"

"Yes."

"Sometimes I hum when I pray."

"You're praying?"

"Yep. A prayer of thanks that we outmaneuvered that jerk."

"A prayer of thanks," he said in a soft, puzzled voice.

"Don't you pray?"

"Never given it much thought."

"That's the beauty of it. You don't have to think about prayer. You just do it."

"Does it help?"

"Absolutely."

She sensed he was processing her explanation. It didn't surprise her that Dr. Spencer wasn't one for prayer. He was a physician, a profession prone to big egos. Some docs didn't feel the need to look outside themselves for guidance, comfort or emotional peace.

"I'm sorry," he said.

"For not listening to me? I get it, you're used to giving orders, not following them."

"Not that. I'm sorry I dragged you into all this."

"Hey, I chose to respond to the call in the mountains."

"But not to do hand-to-hand combat with a psycho in my living room."

"It's good to know I still have my skills. Now shush, we need to listen."

This whole apology and conversation moment in his bedroom felt unusually raw and authentic. She sensed his guard was down, probably because of the head injury, or because of the threatening encounter with the bearded guy. At any rate, a connection was developing between herself and Dr. Spencer, a connection that made her uncomfortable on so many levels.

Maddie had no interest in romance, especially not with a charming city doc she knew would grow tired of country life and flee town soon enough. And Maddie didn't plan on leaving her hometown of Echo Mountain. This was where she belonged.

A crash echoed from the living room. She straightened.

"He broke another window. Determined, isn't he?" she said, positioning herself between the door and Dr. Spencer. She gripped the hiking stick with white-knuckled fingers. If the guy made it into the bedroom, she wouldn't hold back. She'd deliver a full-on assault, the goal being to knock him out.

Could she really do it?

She heard Spence rifling through drawers behind her.

"What are you doing?" she whispered.

"Looking for a weapon."

"I got this."

"I can't sit here and do nothing," Spence said.

Someone jiggled the nickel-plated door handle.

She adjusted her grip on the stick. "Got anything heavy, like a paperweight or rock or something?"

"I've got a salt lamp."

"Get it and stand on the other side of the door. If he breaks in, I'll lure him into the room and you whack him in the head with that thing."

He glanced at the salt lamp in his hand with a distasteful expression. Maiming, killing, was not in his makeup.

Nor was it in hers. But before he'd abandoned her, Dad had taught her the importance of survival, a good thing since that kind of determination could very well save her life tonight.

She and the doctor waited for the assailant's next move. Although Spence seemed fragile, he gripped the eight-inch oblong lamp with resolute focus. She sensed that he, too, would do what was necessary to survive.

"Dear Lord, give us courage," she whispered.

The door handle rattled again, followed by a smacking sound, as if someone was kicking the door.

"And the strength to do what is necessary," she continued.

Whack, whack.

Sirens wailed in the distance, sending a rush of relief through Maddie's chest.

The intruder pounded one last time on the door, probably in frustration, and she heard footsteps echo across the living room.

"He's leaving," Spence said with surprise in his voice. He put down the salt lamp and went to open the door.

"No." She blocked him. "Not yet. Let's wait until we know it's safe."

"Right, okay." He leaned against the wall, blinked a few times and lowered his head.

"Are you light-headed? Dizzy?" She propped the stick against the wall and gripped his arm.

He shook his head and wandered back to the bed. "I'm—"

"Don't say it." She sat beside him on the bed. "We both know you're not fine. Neither am I."

Her phone vibrated. "Hello?"

"We're pulling up now," Chief Walsh said. "Is he in the house?"

"I heard him flee the cabin, but we're staying in the bedroom to be safe."

"I'll let you know when it's clear."

"Thanks." She redirected her attention to Spence.

"This is happening because of me, because I did something that's made me a target, and now you're a target." He caught her gaze for a brief second and then began pacing the room.

"Come on, this isn't your fault," she said.

He paced, rubbing his hands together, growing more agitated. Another symptom of the brain injury?

"What if Officer Carrington is hurt and Gwen doesn't recover?" he said. "What if she dies?"

Maddie had to stop this frantic spin. "Hey, her injury wasn't serious. She's breathing on her own, remember?" She blocked him from pacing to the other side of the room. "Spence?"

"What do you think happened to Red?" he said.

"He's a savvy and strong officer. He'll be okay."

"What if he's wounded? I need to get out there and offer medical assistance."

"Stop." She placed her open palm against his soft cotton

T-shirt. "Remember what they taught you in SAR? Don't become another victim the team has to rescue. Let's wait until we get the clear signal from Nate, then we'll see if Red needs medical assistance."

He turned and paced away from her. She sensed if the armoire wasn't blocking the window he'd climb out and search the property for Red. He wasn't unstable exactly, but he was definitely a tangle of emotions, especially guilt. That seemed irrational, making her question his condition. At times he seemed confused and agitated, and other times he could be totally calm, like when he'd asked her about karate and prayer.

She considered his decision to jump out of hiding to defend Maddie. Was that irrational or sensible? She could make an argument for both sides. It was irrational to expose his location, yet his motivation was pure, born of his protective instinct.

His actions exposed his good heart in wanting to protect Maddie.

Don't go there, Madeline.

"You think I'm crazy, don't you?" he said in a soft voice.

"Why would you say that?"

"The look on your face."

"I was thinking about something else."

The thought of falling in love and being devastated again, because that's what would happen. There hadn't been enough excitement to keep Waylan in town, and there certainly wouldn't be enough to keep a man like Kyle Spencer in Echo Mountain.

He placed a hand on her shoulder. Shocked by his touch, she looked up into his blue eyes.

"I am truly sorry. About everything," he said.

"Stop apologizing. None of this is your fault."

He studied her like he didn't quite believe her words, but wanted to desperately. She also sensed he wanted something else. A hug?

Don't do it, Maddie. The intensity of their situation was

causing a visceral, emotional connection, nothing more. It wasn't real.

"I can't help it," he said. "I hardly know you and yet you've saved my life what, three times now, and in doing so you've risked your own. You didn't sign up for all this. You're just a paramedic."

The sting from his insult must have shown on her face because he put out his hand in a soothing gesture.

"Wait, that didn't come out right."

"Spence! Maddie! Open up!" Chief Walsh called from the living room.

She removed the chair from the door and flung it open. "Good to see you, Chief." With purposeful steps, she crossed the living room to the kitchen.

Just a paramedic? He made it sound like she had an insignificant job in a small, boring town.

The doc's tone reminded her of when Waylan tried talking her into quitting her job claiming she could do so much better. Really? So much better than helping people who were in crisis? She might not be a doctor like Spence or a software engineer like Waylan, but she felt like she was doing God's work, both medically and emotionally, when she was called out on an emergency.

"Maddie," Spence said.

She ignored him, still steaming over his comment.

Ryan, her cop brother, raced into the cabin. "Maddie, you're okay." He hugged her and she welcomed the embrace.

"Did you find Red?" Nate asked Ryan.

Ryan broke the hug. "Sorry, sir. I'll go help check the property."

"I found him," a voice said through the chief's and Ryan's shoulder radios.

Maddie gripped the kitchen counter, bracing herself.

"How is he? Over." Nate said.

"Disoriented and confused from a knock to the head. And he's missing his gun."

* * *

As Spence cracked open his eyes the next morning, he focused on remembering where he was and how he'd ended up here. Wrestling with a disturbing, groundless feeling, he took a few deep breaths to help him recall what had happened.

That's right, Nate made him pack a bag last night and they'd moved Spence to a one-bedroom guest cabin on Echo Mountain Resort property. Spence's own cabin was no longer safe due to broken windows and the fact the attacker could return.

Spence swung his legs off the bed, planted his feet on the floor and glanced around the rustic room with wood-paneled walls. Rubbing his temples, he remembered how things slipped out of his mouth last night past his internal censor—a side effect of his concussion no doubt—so he decided to stop talking. He'd answer direct questions when asked, but otherwise he kept his thoughts to himself.

He remembered the look on Maddie's face when he'd referred to her as *just a paramedic*. That comment certainly didn't come out the way he'd intended. What he'd meant was she wasn't a trained bodyguard and shouldn't have been put in the position of protecting Spence physically against a man twice her size.

Then again, perhaps her misinterpretation of his comment would make her angry enough to keep her distance, because ordering her to leave hadn't worked.

He stood slowly, breathing through the pain of a headache, and slipped into a sweatshirt and jeans. Opening the door, he wandered toward the kitchenette and flipped on an electric hot water kettle. As he glanced out the window over the sink, he remembered the broken windows at the cabin.

"Need to call someone to fix the windows," he muttered to himself.

"Already made the call."

Startled, he spun around and spotted Maddie sitting cross-legged in a thick-cushioned chair with a book open in her lap in the living room. The gas fireplace glowed next to her. She'd gone to battle for him last night and could have been seriously hurt.

"What are you doing here?" The words escaped his lips before they passed through his internal filter. He sounded irritated even to himself, although a part of him was relieved to see her.

She offered a pleasant smile. "Good morning to you, too, grouchy Gus."

He rubbed his forehead. "Sorry. I… I wasn't expecting to see you today."

"The chief asked if I could meet him here to discuss what happened last night. My brother spent the night at my place because I saw the guy's face and he was worried about me. Your protective detail is parked outside. Aiden let me in to wait for the chief. I hope that's okay."

It was more than okay. Not good.

"Is Nate on his way?" He needed her to give her statement and leave as quickly as possible.

He wanted her to stay.

"Nate should be here in about twenty minutes."

"How's Officer Carrington?"

"Concussion, but otherwise okay."

Another person assaulted because of Spence.

"That's not your fault, either," she said.

He turned his back to her, frustrated that she knew what he was thinking. He'd been an expert at masking his feelings and thoughts with a bright smile and friendly demeanor. It was important to keep the mask firmly in place because the confidence in his eyes eased his patients' fears.

Masking his feelings also gave him a sense of control, which right now he desperately needed.

He reached for a mug on the rack and noticed his hand was trembling. Clenching his jaw, he grabbed the mug and placed it on the counter. He wrapped his fingers around the cool ceramic, hoping to stop the trembling. What was the matter with him?

"Tea's up on the left," Maddie said.

He opened a cupboard.

"Your other left," she teased.

He frowned at his own mistake. He knew his left from his right, but felt like he was under a microscope with her watching his every move. A moment later she stepped up beside him.

"I could use a fresh cup of coffee." She pulled a single-serve cup off a carousel and plopped it into the coffeemaker. "These cabins have all the comforts of home."

When she pressed Brew, he noted such delicate fingers on the woman who'd defended him with a hiking stick. He'd never noticed that before, nor had he noticed the faint freckles dotting her nose.

She cocked her head and focused her curious green eyes at him.

"What's that look?" she said.

What could he say? That he was noticing things about her he shouldn't? That he felt vulnerable and appreciated her presence more than she could know?

"I'm hungry." It's all he could come up with.

"Okay." She half-chuckled as if she knew that was not what he was thinking. She opened a drawer and pulled out a paper menu. "I'll order room service."

Spreading the menu out on the countertop, she nibbled at the corner of her lip as she ran her forefinger down the list of breakfast options. "They've got lighter fare like fruit or muffins, or heartier items like oatmeal, or egg scramblers with your choice of meat, veggies and cheese. Oh, and check out the Monster Mash skillet—potatoes, meat, veggies, the works." She cast him a sideways glance. "I'm thinking you're a Monster Mash kinda guy."

"Sounds good." He turned to go sit at the table and she

touched his shirtsleeve. Warmth trickled up his arm to his chest. He wished she wouldn't do that.

"You're not done," she said. "You have to pick ham, sausage or bacon, then cheddar, Swiss, or Colby jack cheese, and there's a list of seven veggies to choose from."

"Too hard. Toast is fine."

He went to the table and sat down, releasing a sigh of tension. Making all those decisions first thing in the morning was stressing him out. It shouldn't, should it? He pressed his fingertips to his temples.

A few seconds later, her grounding hand touched his shoulder. He glanced up. She actually smiled at him. "Do you trust me?"

Trust a woman? What a joke. Yet this wasn't Andrea, it was Maddie McBride, closet ninja, dedicated paramedic and…

Amazing woman.

"You shouldn't have to think that hard, Doc." She frowned.

"I… Sure, you've saved my life. So, yes, I trust you."

"Good, I'll order for you."

He nodded and closed his eyes. She didn't take her hand off his shoulder as she made the call. "This is Maddie McBride in the Juniper Cabin. I'd like to place an order. One Monster Mash with ham, cheddar, spinach and mushrooms, and a bowl of oatmeal with brown sugar and walnuts. Oh, and a side of toast with jam. Great, thanks." She squeezed his shoulder. "It'll be here in thirty to forty minutes."

"Thanks."

"I'll get your tea."

"You shouldn't be waiting on me. You shouldn't even be here." That was uncalled for and so unlike him. She was only trying to help.

He needed to keep his mouth shut.

She slipped her hand off his shoulder and went to get their drinks.

"I'm sorry," he said. "I'm not usually this irritable."

"You're suffering from a head injury, lack of sleep and assorted other aches and pains. You're doing a lot better than I would be under the circumstances."

She returned to the table and placed the mug of tea in front of him. "I hope green lavender is okay."

"It's fine."

She carried her coffee to the chair in the corner. He wished she would sit at the table with him, yet he'd been a jerk again, told her she shouldn't be here. In truth, he'd snapped at her because he hated being damaged in any way, shape or form, and letting her wait on him only drove home how fragile he must seem to everyone.

"What's the book?" he asked, hoping to engage her in conversation.

"Something I found on the shelves." She motioned behind her to a built-in bookcase. "It's a mystery about a woman who buys a bed-and-breakfast, finds a will in the basement and when she investigates, someone tries to kill her."

"Right, because you don't have enough of that in real life," he said.

"Hey, your sense of humor is coming back. Bravo."

"I guess."

"But?"

He shook his head and glanced down. She continued to study him.

A few awkward moments passed as anxiety circled around in his gut.

"Spence?"

When she spoke his name he could hardly ignore her.

"What if…?" he started, fingering the rim of his mug. *Don't say it.*

"What if, what?" she prompted.

"What if I can no longer practice medicine?"

"Because of your head injury?"

He nodded, a ball forming in his throat.

"Hey, the MRI showed a mild concussion, that's all. The swelling will go down and you'll be back to normal soon."

"You and I both know head injuries aren't that simple."

"Maybe not, but you have to think positive. The MRI could have looked a lot worse."

"You don't understand."

"Right, because I'm just a paramedic."

He snapped his attention to her. "That came out wrong last night."

"Then what am I not smart enough to understand?"

"It's not about being smart, which we both know you are. It's about…me."

"A little more, please?"

He sighed. "Without medicine I'm…nothing." Spence's voice cracked.

She stood and crossed the room. He had to look away, didn't want to see the pity in her eyes.

"Look at me," she said, placing a gentle hand against his cheek.

Glancing into her sparkling green eyes, he found himself holding his breath.

"Don't talk that way," she said. "First, you're going to be fine, and second, you're worth a lot more than your job."

He couldn't rip his gaze from her sincere, determined expression. How had he never noticed this woman before, never noticed her natural radiance and positive energy?

Because you weren't in the market for love. Not then, not ever.

"A lot more," she said, her voice taking on a husky edge.

Was she feeling it, too, this arc of emotional connection sparking between them?

Pounding on the cabin door shattered the moment. Maddie snapped her hand away from his face as if she'd nearly gotten it caught in a trap.

"Dr. Spencer!" a woman called.

He started to get up, but Maddie stopped him with a firm hand against his chest.

"I'll get it." She went to the door. "Who's there?"

"Nia Sharpe. It's an emergency!"

Maddie opened the door to the resort's concierge. The patrolman assigned to protect Dr. Spencer hovered beside her.

Nia, who was also Aiden's girlfriend, motioned to Spence. "You've got to do something. It's Aiden. He can't breathe!"

FIVE

Spence's hesitation worried Maddie. It was like his brain was slow to kick into gear.

Maddie snapped into action. "Nia, did you call 9-1-1?"

"Yes."

"What happened?" Spence asked. He motioned for Nia to lead them to Aiden.

"I found him in the barn," Nia said, heading across the property. "He fell or was pushed." She touched Maddie's arm. "Do you think it has something to do with—"

"Let's focus on one thing at a time," Maddie said. "Did you see him fall?"

"No, I was late. I was supposed to help him reorganize the loft, but when I got there he was on the ground, gasping for air and looking at me like...like..."

"Like what?" Spence pressed.

Nia glanced at Spence, tears welling in her eyes. "Like he was scared."

Aiden, scared? Maddie had grown up in her cousin Aiden's house and had never, ever known him to be afraid. Of anything.

Then again, when people were injured and felt vulnerable, they were often overcome with fear, like the fear that had taken hold of Dr. Spencer repeatedly over the past eighteen hours. Fear that his head injury was more serious than it looked; fear that he'd never practice medicine again. Maddie's heart ached for the man.

When they reached the barn, Maddie rushed to Aiden's side. "Aiden, can you hear me?"

He gasped for breath, his blue eyes widening with panic. Dr. Spencer knelt on the other side of him. The police officer assigned to Spence stayed close.

"What do you think, Doctor?" Nia asked.

When he didn't respond right away, Maddie said, "Let's rule out the obvious."

Spence glanced at Maddie.

"Diaphragm spasm," she said.

"Of course," he agreed.

"What does that mean?" Nia said.

"Simply put, he got the wind knocked out of him," Maddie said.

She and Spence pulled Aiden's knees up to his abdomen. Maddie watched her cousin's reaction.

"What are you doing?" Nia said.

"Trying to relax his abdominal muscles," Maddie explained. "Aiden, can you breathe slowly in through the nose and out through your mouth?"

He did as ordered and she found herself pretending he wasn't her cousin because the look of panic on his face was making her stomach twist into knots. She could definitely understand why Nia, who'd fallen deeply in love with Aiden, was so upset.

"You think that's all it is?" Nia said, directing the question to Dr. Spencer.

"We can't be sure until he's checked out at the hospital and they take some X-rays," he said.

Good, a professional, doctor-like answer. Maybe Spence was coming around and remembering everything that he could do.

"I'll check his pulse." Dr. Spencer pressed his fingers to

Aiden's wrist and glanced at his own watch, another sign that the fog was lifting.

"Aiden?" Maddie said. "Breathe in slowly, buddy, that's it. And then out…" she coached.

The sound of a wailing siren cut through the tension.

"Nia, go get the paramedics," Maddie said.

Nia raced out of the barn.

"It's 110," Spence said.

It could be high due to anxiety. Spence must have thought the same thing.

"Aiden, you're doing great, buddy," Spence said. "We think you've had the wind knocked out of you. Keep breathing with Maddie."

Aiden looked at Maddie.

"You heard it from the doc," Maddie said. "Breathe and relax."

"Hey, what are you doing here?" Rocky said, rushing into the barn with the cute paramedic named Vivian pushing the back end of the stretcher. Rocky's smile faded when he saw Dr. Spencer.

Rocky knelt beside Maddie. "Pulse?"

"A hundred and ten," the doctor answered.

"We got this," Rocky said in dismissal.

Dr. Spencer stood slowly with an odd expression on his face. Was he offended that Rocky was taking over? Or relieved? Sometimes he was hard to read.

Nate rushed into the barn. "What happened?"

"We don't know," Nia said. "He fell or was pushed—"

"Pushed?"

"He's the most coordinated person I know," Nia said. "He wouldn't have fallen off the loft."

They glanced up at the fifteen-foot drop.

"I got here as soon as I could." Scott Beckett, the resort's security manager and Bree's boyfriend, joined the group. "How is he?"

Rocky glared at Maddie. "Really?" he said, irritated by all the people hovering over him.

"Let's give them some space." Maddie herded the group toward the exit. She realized she was missing one. Glancing over her shoulder, she noticed Spence still standing by the paramedics.

"Spence?" she said.

"But…" He hesitated, watching Rocky and Vivian tend to Aiden. "I'm a doctor."

Rocky shook his head, offended by the comment.

"You're off duty," Maddie said. "Come on, let them do their job."

Spence didn't move for a second. A cold chill skittered across Maddie's shoulders. She didn't want to think it, but couldn't help herself—the doc's brain injury was, in fact, more serious than anyone suspected. What else would make him seem so lost?

No, she wouldn't go there. Once the swelling went down, patients with brain injuries could spring right back to normal, no problem. They didn't necessarily suffer long-lasting effects and were able to reenter their lives without missing a beat.

As Dr. Spencer stepped away from Aiden, Maddie touched his arm. "Good thing we were here."

"Yeah." Was that sarcasm lacing his voice? If so, that meant he had the presence of mind to know he wasn't functioning at one hundred percent.

Chief Walsh, who was questioning Nia outside, waved them over. "Did he give you any indication he thought someone was around, that he felt threatened?"

"By the time I got to him he couldn't speak," Nia said.

"Hey, he's tough. He'll be okay," Scott encouraged. Nia nodded, but didn't look convinced.

The paramedics rolled Aiden out of the barn on the stretcher and Nia rushed to his side, walking with him to the ambulance. Maddie suspected Aiden's injuries weren't serious, yet Nia's reaction tore at her insides.

As they headed back to the cabin, Maddie wondered if she'd ever experience that kind of profound love, that kind of connection with a man. She'd thought she'd had it with Waylan. As teenagers he'd helped her through some of the darkest days of her life after Dad left, Mom withdrew emotionally, and then even she moved away. Waylan's love had been the beacon of light that sparked hope for Maddie each and every day.

Then Waylan had abandoned her for a more exciting life in the city.

"What is it?"

She snapped her attention to Dr. Spencer. "What?"

"Your expression—it's rather sad."

"I'm fine."

She sensed he knew she wasn't fine at all.

They returned to the small cabin and Nate shut the door. "The officer will remain posted outside."

Maddie wandered to the kitchen table and grabbed her mug of coffee. She'd slept poorly last night in her apartment, the violence of the day invading her dreams. At two in the morning she'd finally given up, knelt beside her bed and prayed. Prayer always calmed her runaway thoughts.

As Nate poured himself a cup of coffee, Spence leaned against the counter. "Anything on the bearded man from last night?"

"Why don't you take a seat?" Nate motioned to the kitchen table.

Maddie and Spence joined him. Nate cleared his voice as if hesitating to share bad news.

"I don't like the sound of that," Spence said.

"And I don't like anything about this case. Gwen gave me her statement. She never sent you the text message asking for help."

"Wait, but the message came from her phone," Spence said.

"She lost her phone a few days ago. She used a find-your-phone app, which led her into the mountains. She struggled with the assailant and fell."

"So a guy I don't know gets ahold of Gwen's phone and sends me a text to lure me into the mountains to what? Kill me?"

"It's looking that way." Nate leaned forward. "You need to seriously consider making a list of potential enemies."

Spence shook his head in frustration.

"The sooner you figure out who's after you the quicker your life can get back to normal," Maddie offered.

"Work on that list, Spence," Nate said.

"I wouldn't know where to start."

"Right, because Dr. Dreamboat has no enemies," Maddie said.

"None that are angry enough to want me dead."

"You may not realize how angry they are," Nate said. "What about dissatisfied patients or family members who disagreed with your course of treatment? Someone from your past?"

"I'll help him get started," Maddie said.

"Good, thanks," Nate said, and then redirected his attention to Spence. "I need you to remember if the guy said anything last night that could help us figure out who he is."

Spence glanced at Maddie, then back at Nate.

She sensed he didn't want to say something in front of her. Well, tough beans. She wasn't leaving.

"I remembered something this morning," Spence said. "The man said 'you'll pay for your sins.'"

Nate frowned. "What sins?"

Spence stared into his coffee. Shame twisted his features, but shame about what?

"What is it?" Maddie pressed.

Spence snapped his attention to her. "Nothing."

"Spence?" Nate said.

"What do you want me to say?" He stood suddenly and

gripped his head. "I need to lie down." He marched into the bedroom and shut the door.

Nate shared a concerned look with Maddie. "I'm worried about him."

"He'll be okay. He's sore and frustrated that he isn't working, ya know, saving lives."

Nate eyed the bedroom door. "He doesn't seem like himself. What do you think's going on?"

"Sorry, but I don't know him that well."

"You see him all the time at the hospital."

"I hand off patients and leave. The doc and I have rarely spoken for any length of time, well, until yesterday."

"But you know how positive he usually is, how upbeat and happy. This guy…" He shook his head. "I'm not sure I know this guy."

"It's still Dr. Spencer. You've never seen him wounded and worried. He's really worried."

"That's good. That means he's taking the threat against his life seriously."

That wasn't what Maddie had meant. Spence was terrified that his life was over because he'd be benched from practicing medicine.

"I wasn't done discussing the case," Nate said.

"He should rest if he feels he needs it. I can text you when he awakens."

"Are you staying all day?"

"Maybe, if you think it's a good idea."

"Definitely. Having a medical professional close by gives me peace of mind. I'm not sure about Spence's judgment right now."

Spence was hiding. There was no other way to describe it. As he lay in bed staring at the ceiling, he realized he was hiding from everything: regrets from the past, Nate's probing questions, the possibility he might have made enemies angry enough to want him dead, and the unnerving feeling that he was never safe.

Except when Maddie was close.

He sat up. It was unfair to put her danger, and he wasn't a coward by nature, yet the few hours of rest had eased his headache and made him feel almost normal, like his old self.

His typically charming self would be quick to forge ahead with his life. Figuring out who was after him was the first step. His usual self would also be quick to apologize to Maddie for his sharp tone. She knew he was struggling and yet she'd covered for him in the barn when they'd assessed and treated Aiden. She was Spence's closest confidant at this point. He should appreciate her efforts, not take her for granted.

Or push her away.

His phone vibrated with a call from Dr. Carver. He cleared his throat, needing to sound strong, confident.

"Hi, Ruth, how are you?" he said in the most charming voice he could manage.

"You sound better."

"I am better, thanks. What's the word on Aiden McBride?"

"Bruised tailbone and mild concussion. Apparently he was reaching for something and lost his balance. I heard you were there when it happened?"

"Yes, Nate put me up in a cabin at the resort because of the break-in at my place last night."

"Oh, Spence. How frightening."

"I'm okay. Safe at the resort under police protection."

"Which cabin are you staying in? I'll send the assistant over to the resort."

"Actually, let's not involve anyone else at this point. Chief Walsh thinks it could be personal, that someone might be after me, so the fewer people in my orbit the better."

"Spence, I'm sorry."

"Thanks."

"Do you have any idea who it could be?"

"None. A disgruntled patient perhaps, or someone who thinks I've wronged him?"

"But everyone loves you here."

"I'm sure not everyone."

"Well, let me know if there's anything I can do to help. In the meantime, get well and I'll take you off the schedule until further notice."

He didn't like the sound of that.

"I'd still like to work once I'm up to it."

Silence answered him.

"Ruth?"

"Spence, you just told me someone is after you. Do you think it wise to bring that kind of danger to the hospital?"

"No, but—"

"I'm surprised you made the suggestion."

He heard the message behind her words: any logical-thinking person, not suffering from brain trauma, would have better sense than to talk about coming back to work and bringing trouble with him.

"Just didn't want you to forget about me," he joked. "How's Gwen?"

"Vitals are good. She's out of the woods. You did excellent work out there, Dr. Spencer."

"Tell her I said hi."

"I will. And don't worry about your patients or staffing. Take as much time off as necessary, months if you need it. You've earned it."

"Thanks."

He ended the call and stared at the phone in his hand. Months off work? He'd lose his mind.

The stress of being cooped up in a one-bedroom cabin and not doing his life's work sparked another headache. He couldn't stand feeling useless.

Helpless.

He glanced out the window at the rain falling from the

gray sky. The darkness matched his mood. He had to stop denying the possibility that someone was targeting him, and figure out the identity of his tormentor.

If he couldn't convince Maddie to distance herself he might as well join forces with her to investigate who was after him. She was a bright woman with a calming nature who didn't seem interested in a romantic entanglement like the other ladies in town.

He opened the bedroom door and glanced across the cabin at the chair where she had been sitting earlier. It was empty.

He was alone.

Disappointment fell heavy across his shoulders. He hadn't realized how much he appreciated her presence until just now.

Going to the kitchen area, he opened the refrigerator and was greeted by a dozen or so casserole dishes, plastic containers and fresh juices. He spotted a white container and cracked it open. It looked like the breakfast Maddie had ordered him.

The cabin door opened. "Hey, you're awake." Carrying two large bags in her arms, Maddie toed the door shut behind her.

"Let me help," he offered.

"Actually, I'm perfectly balanced." Her lips curled into a pleasant smile. The tension eased across his shoulders. She slid the bags onto the counter and cracked open the refrigerator. "I was afraid of that."

"Where did it all come from?"

She raised an eyebrow. "Like you don't know."

"I don't, honest."

"All your lady admirers." She began rearranging the food and adding to it from her grocery bags. "The whole town knows about last night's break-in and that you're temporarily homeless."

"Wait, I'm not sure it's a good idea for people to know I'm here."

"They don't know you're in the Juniper Cabin, only that you're at the resort. Saving Aiden this morning got everyone talking."

"You did more of the saving than I did."

She pinned him with those incredible green eyes. "Yeah, what was that about?"

He crossed his arms over his chest. "I froze. That's never happened to me before."

"You're still recovering," she said, as if that was an acceptable answer. "In the mood for lunch? I brought brain food so we could focus on the EP."

"Extended play?" he questioned.

"Enemy project."

"Ah, right. I'll eat my Monster Mash as long as it's here."

She shut the refrigerator door and looked at him. "I want you to know, nothing you say to me leaves this cabin. You can trust me, Doctor—" She caught herself. "Spence."

They spent the afternoon making a list of potential enemies, although not the entire afternoon. Maddie encouraged Spence to lie down a few times because she sensed the strain was irritating his headache. How did she do that? How did she know what he was thinking? How he was feeling?

They also took a break to meet with a forensic artist. Spence and Maddie came up with a pretty good likeness of the bearded man who broke into the cabin last night.

Maddie had set up a whiteboard on the kitchen counter where they listed five potential enemies. He shared the odd, threatening emails he'd been receiving, and when she glanced at each one she crinkled her nose in concentration. The expression would be adorable if it wasn't her way of focusing on the threat against Spence's life.

"This one is awfully cryptic. 'Your mistake has become my destiny.' What's that mean?"

"Haven't a clue."

Maddie pointed to the whiteboard. "Any of these people could consider your behavior a mistake. For instance, Roger Grimes holds a grudge because you reported suspected abuse of his fourteen-year-old daughter, Megan. Was reporting him a mistake?"

"Last I heard, Children's Services was still investigating."

"And Anthony Price is upset with you because…?"

"His fiancée, Theresa, and I had coffee in the cafeteria a few times."

"And Anthony thinks it was more than just coffee?"

"I've heard Theresa has a crush on me. I can't control that."

"No, of course not," she teased.

"Why are you needling me?"

"Sorry, it's that whole, 'you've gotta laugh about it so you don't cry about it' thing. Humor is an awesome coping mechanism."

"What have you used it to cope with?"

"Family stuff. Let's focus." She pointed to a name. "Why is Lucas Winfield on the list?"

"He's a seventeen-year-old kid that was brought in with hallucinations. He ingested an overdose of edible cannabis. I know it's legal in Washington, but not until you're twenty-one. I reported it to Nate."

"Lucas isn't going to try to hurt you over that, is he?"

"His parents were so upset they sent him to military school. He ran away. I hear he's still missing."

"Whoa, I didn't know about that."

"The parents are keeping the running away part quiet. I guess they felt responsible on some level."

"The burdens we carry," she sighed.

"What burdens do you carry, Maddie McBride?"

She turned to him from the whiteboard. "Nothing I can't handle with prayer and humor."

He wanted to question her more, but suspected she would deflect again, wanting to finish his list.

"Who's the Tomlin family?" she asked.

"Oliver Tomlin died in my ER back in Portland from medication complications. No one told us he was on a certain medication that interacted with the nitroglycerin we gave him for chest pain. His blood pressure dropped so low he died of a heart attack." Spence shook his head. "So frustrating. Either his wife, Tina, didn't know he was on the drug, or she chose not to tell us for some reason."

"That's sad."

"I heard that family fell apart after Oliver's death."

"You heard?"

"I left my position in Portland a few months after he died, but an associate of mine keeps me posted, as does the hospital administrator. The Tomlins sued the hospital for wrongful death. The courts dismissed the suit."

"Okay." She stepped back. "That's a pretty solid list, but haven't you left someone out?" She quirked an eyebrow at him.

"I don't think so."

"What about Dr. Danner?"

"William? He's harmless. A lot of bark, but no bite. Kind of like a Yorkie."

Maddie burst out laughing and pride swelled in his chest. He'd done that. In the midst of all this darkness, he'd made her laugh. Spence wanted to do it again, tomorrow, the next day and the day after that.

She composed herself and sat with him at the kitchen table, still eyeing the whiteboard. He might feel proud that he'd made her laugh, but he couldn't afford to get used to having her around all the time.

Even though he wanted her around. All the time.

It was nearly dinnertime and he considered asking her to stay for a meal. He had plenty of food.

"Aunt Margaret is in a knitting club with Anthony's grandmother, so perhaps she can get the scoop on his state of mind, and I think cousin Bree is friends with Lucas's aunt, Beth. Maybe she can find out what's going on with Lucas. You focus on the Tomlins."

"I think we should give the list to Nate."

"We will, but not everyone likes talking to the police. Nate can check the status of the abuse charge against Roger, and it would be nice to know where Dr. Danner was when Gwen went looking for her phone. I don't trust the guy. Ruling out Dr. Nasty should be our first step."

"Dr. Nasty, huh? Do we all have nicknames?"

"Pretty much. So, we're good?"

He'd be better if she'd stay for dinner.

She glanced at him.

"Yes, we're good," he said.

Do you want to have dinner with me? The words got caught in his throat. What was the matter with him? He wasn't fifteen asking a girl on a first date.

Which was exactly the point. He shouldn't be inviting Maddie to dinner given their current situation. Wasn't he the one who'd wanted her to keep her distance?

Her phone beeped with a text and she glanced at it. "I'd better go."

"Yes, that's a good idea."

She glanced at him. "Sick of me already, huh?"

"Not exactly, but it's time you leave."

She didn't move to get up. Studying him intently, she said, "You're trying to get rid of me. What's wrong? Is it your head? Do your ribs hurt? What do you need?"

Way too much to ask of her.

"I'm fine."

"I've stopped hearing you when you use those words. Try again."

"There's no reason for you to stay." He figured being so direct would drive her away.

She shot him a side glance. "What are you up to?"

"Excuse me?"

"You seem intent on me leaving. What did you do, text one of your lady friends to come over for dinner?" she teased.

Of course he didn't, but he couldn't tell Maddie the truth, that he was developing feelings for her.

"Ooohhh, you really did." She stood and grabbed her purse. "I hope you cleared that with Nate."

"Maddie—"

"I get it, I do." She cut him off. "You deserve more stimulating social interaction beyond me grilling you about your enemies."

"Did you want something to eat before you go?" he said, feeling incredibly awkward. "I've got plenty."

"Nah, your lady admirers made that food for you." Maddie headed toward the door. "Enjoy it with your date. I'm staying at Bree's cottage across the way if you need anything."

"She lives here?"

"She's the grounds manager for the resort, so they set her up in a cottage on the property. You've got my cell number."

"I appreciate it. I don't know how I'd manage without you."

She turned to him. "What did you say?"

"I appreciate it."

"The other part."

"I don't know how I'd manage without you?"

"Wow, a compliment. I'm not sure what to do with that," she teased. "My brother's got protective duty right outside, so you're safe, okay?"

He nodded. Wanted to say something. Couldn't.

"Have a good night." She closed the door behind her.

Spence rushed across the cabin, stopping mere inches from the door. What was he doing? She was gone. He wanted her to leave, to get some time off from babysitting him.

A part of him wanted to call out, to thank her again for saving his life.

He couldn't possibly thank her enough.

She deserved to hear his sincere thanks, but he'd been so careful not to cross the line, not to give her any signals that he was interested in her other than as a partner in crime prevention.

As he stood there, staring at the door, he wondered what made him think she had any inclination in that direction. For all he knew the rumors could be true about her and Rocky, that they were secretly in love but they couldn't make it public or one of them would have to resign from work.

Regardless of her dating situation, Spence owed her a debt of gratitude, and letting her assume a woman was joining him for dinner seemed to bother her just now. He could read it in her eyes. He'd moved past trying to constantly push her away and felt like he owed her an apology.

He flung the door open. "Maddie?"

Spence peered into the dark night, but she was gone. He strained to see her. How was that possible? She'd left only moments ago.

"Maddie!" he called out, louder this time.

Silence echoed back at him. He glanced toward her sister's cottage, but didn't see Maddie's silhouette crossing the property.

"What are you doing?" Maddie's voice echoed.

He snapped his head left.

"Let go!" she said.

Spence took off toward the sound without a jacket or hat. He didn't feel the cold, not when panic was lighting him from the inside.

A car engine roared to life.

Spence caught sight of taillights speeding away.

"Maddie!" he called after the vehicle, but it was too far away.

From his peripheral vision he saw a second car speeding toward him. Closer, closer…

SIX

A black SUV screeched to a stop, blocking Spence. Officer Ryan McBride, Maddie's brother, jumped out. "What are you doing, Dr. Spencer?"

"Your sister," he said, trying to catch his breath. "Someone took her." Spence pointed, but the car had turned the corner.

Ryan glanced at Resort Drive, then back at Spence. "Are you sure?"

Still breathing heavily, Spence nodded, the exertion threatening to spike another headache.

"I think you're confused. Maddie went to Bree's. Come on, I'll show you."

"No, someone took her!" Spence shouted.

Ryan put out his hand in a calming gesture. "Doc, relax, she texted me. She's okay."

Spence frowned. Could he be mistaken? Or was he completely losing it?

"I heard her voice," he said. "Demanding someone let her go."

"Come on." Officer McBride motioned Spence to his truck.

Spence climbed into the passenger seat and they drove the short distance to the cottage in silence. The police officer probably thought Spence had gone completely nuts, or at the very least he wondered why Spence was so worried about Maddie.

They knocked on the cottage door and Bree answered, holding back her golden retriever.

"Oh, hi. I thought you were Maddie," she said.

"You mean she's not here?" Ryan said.

"She's on her way."

Ryan looked at Spence. "Make and model of the car."

"It was too far away, but I think it was a small pickup."

"What's going on?" Bree said, her eyes rounding.

"Someone took Maddie," Spence explained.

"We don't know that for sure," Ryan said. "She could have gone off with a friend."

"It didn't sound like a friendly interaction," Spence said.

Ryan ripped his phone off his belt.

"Come on in." Bree motioned to them.

Spence and Ryan joined her inside. Ryan paced the front hallway as he called Maddie. "Answer the phone," he muttered.

"Text her," Spence said.

"She could be helping a friend." Bree glanced at Spence. "She's always there when they need her."

Didn't he know it.

Ryan stared at his phone, waiting. A moment later he glanced up. "She's not responding to my text."

"Let me try." Bree slipped her phone out of her pocket and sent a message. "An SOS will get her attention." She sent her message and glanced at Ryan, offering a supportive smile.

But seconds stretched into minutes, and there was still no response from Maddie.

Ryan reached for his shoulder radio. "I'm calling the chief."

"Rocky, give me my phone," Maddie demanded, adjusting herself in the front seat of his truck.

"Come on, can't you live without it for two minutes?"

"You make it sound like I have a problem."

He shot her a side glance as he pulled onto the highway.

"I don't have a problem," she protested.

"Yeah, right."

"You're enjoying this, being in control."

He handed her the phone. "That's not what it's about."

"What then?"

"It's about you looking out for yourself for a change."

"Uh, I've been taking care of myself for ten years, since Mom moved away."

"Try again."

"You're not making any sense."

"You put everyone else first, your brother, friends, and now that arrogant doctor."

"Why do you dislike him so much?"

"He was never your favorite person in the world, either."

"True, but I appreciate him for helping save my cousin last year."

"And by luring the bad guys away from Cassie, Dr. Dreamboat increases his hero status," he muttered.

"I don't think he was doing it for hero status."

"You sound like you know the guy. No one knows him, not really. His smile hides something dark and tragic. You were the one who said that."

"Since the assault in the mountains I've seen another side of him."

"Wonderful," Rocky said, sarcastic.

She glanced out the window. "Where are we going?"

"Healthy Eats. I'm buying you dinner."

"I'd better text Bree."

He shot her a look.

"It's rude not to let her know I won't be home for dinner. Although, I could bring her something."

"Home? The cottage isn't your home, Maddie. Why are you staying there anyway?"

"It's convenient."

"You mean it's close to Dr. Dreamboat."

"You are really busting my chops tonight."

"Because I worry about you."

Maddie sighed. This was probably why folks thought she and Rocky were a couple. He always seemed so solicitous and caring. Then a thought struck her: Could he truly be in love with her? No, she couldn't go there right now.

She glanced at her phone and noticed a missed call and text from her overprotective brother, and a text from Bree.

Worried about you.

She texted a response to both of them.

I'm fine.

She pocketed her phone and turned to Rocky. "I thought you had a date tonight."

"Blew me off."

They pulled into the crowded parking lot of the town's most popular restaurant. Once inside Healthy Eats, Nate's sister Catherine, the owner, greeted them.

"Hi, guys," she said. "I've got a booth in the corner or a few spots at the counter."

A booth sounded romantic and Maddie didn't want to give Rocky the wrong idea. Maybe it was time they had *that* discussion.

"What do you think?" he said.

"Counter's fine."

He motioned her ahead and they found seats. Catherine was quick to serve their drinks. Coffee for Rocky and hot chocolate for Maddie.

"I'll see what Bree wants for dinner." She pulled out her phone and texted her cousin.

"You could order it while we're eating, then it'll be hot when you get back to her place."

"Good plan. It will probably take her a few minutes to look at the menu online anyway." She pocketed her phone and gazed into a mirror behind the counter. She spotted a few local residents eyeing Rocky and Maddie sitting together. The rumors were certainly going to fly by morning.

She turned to him. "Can I talk to you about something?"

"What's up?" he said, blowing on his hot coffee.

"We're friends, right?"

He glanced at her with furrowed brows. "Is that a trick question?"

"Be honest."

"Haven't I always been?"

In that moment, as she studied the curious expression on his handsome face, she realized he would make a wonderful husband someday. Just not for her.

"Dr. Carver made a comment about you and me being, ya know, a couple," she said.

"And how did you respond to that one?"

"I didn't know how to respond. I was shocked."

He stared into his mug of coffee. "Right."

So it was true. He cared about her as more than a friend.

"Oh," she said. "I'm sorry."

He shrugged. "I get it. I know how much Waylan hurt you when he left." Then he looked straight into her eyes. "I would never hurt you, Maddie, ever."

"I know you wouldn't. You're my very best friend."

A sad smile eased across his lips. "Ouch."

She wanted to say more. She wanted to apologize that she didn't have romantic feelings for him. Had Waylan emotionally damaged her so badly that she was incapable of falling in love with a kind man?

No, she wasn't broken or damaged. She just wasn't attracted to Rocky like that.

Like she was attracted to Dr. Spencer.

She stirred her hot chocolate, frustrated. Would she always be destined to fall for the wrong guy? Either ambitious men who put their careers before love, like Waylan, or enigmas like Spence?

Although Rocky was acting a little bossy tonight, he was generally kind and funny. The doctor, on the other hand, had been challenging and moody since the assault, and before that he'd always seemed aloof bordering on arrogant.

The absolute wrong kind of guy with whom to build a life. Maddie wanted stability, not chaos.

She glanced at Rocky. If only…

But she didn't feel that way about him. Now that the question was out in the open she hoped it wouldn't ruin their friendship.

"You are very special to me," she said.

"Apparently not special enough."

"Rocky, you're a great guy but—"

"Let's leave it at 'Rocky, you're a great guy.'" He cracked a half smile. "It's okay." He redirected his attention into his coffee. "But a piece of unsolicited advice? At some point you have to move on."

"You mean past the heartbreak?"

He nodded. "Maybe even start a life somewhere outside Echo Mountain."

"Why? I like it here."

"As long as you're here because you want to be here, not because you're afraid to leave." He glanced at her. "Or because you're waiting for them to come back."

"Them?"

"Waylan." He paused. "And your parents."

She stirred her hot chocolate, thoughtful. Was it true? Was she afraid to leave, to move on with her life? Did a part of her cling to her extended family and friends in Echo Mountain because she was secretly hoping the people she loved would return?

"I'm sorry if I offended you," he said.

"You didn't."

Sirens drew her attention outside. Two police cars pulled into the lot, lights flashing.

A few seconds later, the front doors opened and her brother stormed into the restaurant followed by the police chief and Dr. Spencer. Her heart skipped a beat.

Ryan's cheeks flared bright red as he approached her. The doc's expression was unreadable. She shifted off her stool, panicked. "What happened?"

Ryan opened his mouth and shut it again, as if he struggled to form words.

"Ryan, tell me," she demanded.

"Let's take this outside." Nate motioned for her and Rocky to join them.

Privacy was a good idea considering the diners filling the restaurant. As they marched to the door, her heart hammered against her chest. Was it Aunt Margaret? Bree? Was Aiden's condition worse than they thought?

Nate motioned them toward his patrol car. Ryan suddenly turned and shot dagger eyes at Rocky, and then glared at Maddie. "What's going on here?"

That judgmental, accusatory tone set her teeth on edge. "We were eating dinner," she said as if it was the most obvious answer in the world.

"You disappeared and didn't answer my call," Ryan snapped.

"I texted that I was fine."

"You took her against her will," Dr. Spencer directed at Rocky.

"I think your head injury is messing with your judgment, Doc."

"Rocky," Maddie admonished.

"What? He's accusing me of kidnapping you. That's crazy."

"I heard Maddie say, 'Let go of me,'" Spence said. "She obviously didn't want to go with you."

"And then you ignored me and didn't respond immediately to Bree's text," Ryan added. "With everything that's going on? Really, Maddie?"

"Let's all take a breath," Nate said. "Maddie, what happened after you left Dr. Spencer tonight?"

"I was walking to Bree's cottage and Rocky pulled up." She glanced at the doctor. "Rocky grabbed the strap of my bag and pulled me into his truck, which is why I said 'let go.'"

"So you did not go willingly?" Spence said.

"He was being playful. Not forceful. You must have misunderstood."

"At least you're okay," Ryan shook his head and turned toward his cruiser. "Come on, Doc."

Spence didn't move. It was like he was waiting for Maddie, that he wasn't going anywhere unless she was with him. She surely didn't want to ride in the patrol car with her brother and suffer through an angry lecture.

"Chief, I'm really sorry about this," Maddie said. "I had no idea going to dinner with Rocky would cause such a misunderstanding. I was about to order food to take to Bree. Can I still do that? Rocky can drive me to Bree's cottage."

"I'll wait and give you an escort," Nate said. "Spence, go on back with Officer McBride."

"I'd rather wait for Maddie," Spence said.

With a frustrated sigh, Rocky marched back into the restaurant.

"Officer McBride," Nate said. "Head back to the resort. I'll bring Dr. Spencer and Maddie."

"Yes, sir," he said, getting into his cruiser.

"Ryan, I'm sorry," Maddie called out.

Her brother slammed the door shut.

"Go ahead and order the food," Nate said to Maddie. "We'll wait for you out here."

With a nod, Maddie turned toward the restaurant, frustrated that Rocky's good intentions had caused such tension between her and her brother.

"Maddie?" Spence said.

She glanced over her shoulder at him.

"I'm glad you're okay," he said.

Maddie had barely spoken to Spence on the ride back to the resort. He assumed she was upset that he'd overreacted about her disappearance. He'd apologized to her in the squad car, but Nate said Spence did the right thing.

"It's always better to be vigilant than to ignore your gut," Nate said.

Maddie stared out the window.

In this case, Spence's gut had been wrong. Maddie hadn't been in danger. She'd been out with her work partner. It bothered Spence that she'd refused to have dinner with him, yet went off with Rocky.

When Spence asked her why she'd ignored her brother's call, she explained that she'd been in a heated discussion with Rocky and figured responding to her brother and cousin via text would suffice. She said that Rocky had been trying to make a point: Maddie always put everyone else first, but never herself.

The car went silent after that comment as if she was ashamed, that caring so much about others was a personality flaw.

It wasn't a flaw. It was a gift. Hadn't she put Spence's welfare above her own ever since they'd found Gwen on the trail?

Nate dropped Maddie off at her cousin's cottage and took Spence to the cabin where Ryan waited. Spence apologized to Maddie's brother for overreacting, but the officer said it wasn't necessary, that his irresponsible sister should have answered his call and texted more than a simple "I'm fine."

Spence wanted to argue the "irresponsible" remark, but thought better of it. As he and Ryan ate dinner, Spence learned that Ryan felt very protective of Maddie, which drove her crazy because she considered herself an independent woman.

He and Ryan watched TV for an hour and Spence turned in early.

Even now, well past midnight, he was unable to sleep. Perhaps another symptom of his concussion, or he could be wired from tonight's excitement. So worried about Maddie being kidnapped, he'd caught himself praying for her safety.

Hang on, praying?

Spence shook his head and rolled onto his back, staring at the ceiling. The lights were off in his room, but the full moon glowed through the sheer curtains.

He felt incredibly alone, detached from everyone. The brain trauma was messing with him again, making him moody and sullen. He wasn't alone; he had plenty of friends.

Then again real friends would know the truth about the patient he'd lost in Portland, about Spence's brother who'd died at only eight years old. True friends would know about his fiancée's betrayal that cut him so deeply he'd become an expert at keeping people at a distance with his effusive charm and practiced smile.

Well, he'd kept everyone at a distance except Maddie. She'd somehow seen right through his facade.

He started to drift, recalling how Maddie talked him down from his precarious ledge after the attack in the hospital; remembering the lovely image of her curled up on the chair in the cabin. It helped to visualize that image, a content and peaceful Maddie reading a book close by.

Then the images turned violent, images of his enemy coming for him.

Coming for Maddie.

He jackknifed in bed, his heart pounding. Needing to distract himself, he slipped on a sweatshirt and opened his bedroom door. Officer McBride was sitting at the kitchen table looking at his phone.

"Shouldn't you be asleep?" he asked.

"Not happening anytime soon." Spence wandered to the kitchen counter and made some tea. He motioned to the table. "Mind if I...?"

"Sure, have a seat. I was reading a book on my phone."

"About your 'irresponsible sister' comment earlier..." Spence started.

"That was harsh. I was upset," Ryan said, putting his phone in his pocket. "She's so frustrating sometimes, but I love her."

"Frustrating how?"

"Stubborn, opinionated. I think it's a defense mechanism."

Spence glanced at Ryan in question.

"She's dealt with her share of pain," Ryan continued. "Dad left us when she was fourteen and I was seventeen. Mom fell apart and Maddie tried so hard to make it better, to make Mom better. But you can't fix other people, ya know?"

Spence nodded that he understood. He remembered how he'd wanted to help his own parents deal with their grief after Bobby had died, but at thirteen, Spence had no clue what to do.

"Anyway, when Maddie was fifteen Mom moved away to be with a cousin in Florida. Didn't exactly invite her teenage daughter along," Ryan continued. "So Maddie moved in with Aunt Margaret. Maddie loves our aunt and cousins, but it's not the same. I think she felt like it was her fault somehow that my folks left."

"That's tough on a teenager."

"Yeah, and then there was the idiot boyfriend." Ryan shook his head.

"A jerk?"

"Actually he was really good for her. Brought her out of her funk."

Jealousy tweaked in Spence's chest. "Then why is he an idiot?"

"He moved away for school and basically dropped out of her life. It was traumatic." Ryan glanced at Spence. "I think that's what makes her Maddie, the bullheaded woman who will never leave Echo Mountain."

"She won't leave because…?"

"She'll never run away like my parents and Waylan."

"You can move away and not be running from something."

"Yeah, try telling her that."

Spence considered Ryan's words.

"Anyway, I know I overreacted when she disappeared with Rocky, but it's that big brother thing, which is unnecessary because she is one strong woman." A proud smile eased across his lips.

He had every right to be proud of his sister. Spence was not only proud, but also incredibly grateful.

The peaceful moment was shattered by a shrill alarm coming from the resort.

Ryan pushed back his chair and went to the front window.

"What's going on?" Spence said.

"Not sure. Dispatch," he said into his radio. "You get a call for an alarm at Echo Mountain Resort?"

"Affirmative. Engine 52 and ambulance are on the way."

"A fire?" Ryan asked.

"Affirmative."

Someone pounded on the cabin door.

"It's Nia!" a muffled voice cried.

Ryan opened the door to the hotel's concierge wearing a frantic expression.

"Fire truck and ambulance are on the way," Ryan said.

"We can't wait. There's a fire in the kitchen. They think a little girl is inside. We need your help."

"Let's go." Spence approached the door.

Ryan blocked him. "No, we've got orders."

"It'll take emergency five to seven minutes to get here," Spence said. "We can't wait."

Ryan considered for a second. "I'll call the chief."

"Call him on the way." Spence grabbed a jacket and marched out of the cabin. "Where's Aiden?" he asked Nia.

"I paged him. He might be wiped out from the fall today. Went to bed early? I don't know."

As Spence, Nia and Ryan jogged across the property, Ryan radioed that they were assisting with rescue efforts. By the time they reached the south entrance, guests had evacuated the resort and smoke was seeping out of the kitchen windows.

Ryan approached a small group of employees who were hovering by the entrance. "Everyone okay?"

They all nodded that they were.

"I'm Edith, head cook," a middle-aged woman introduced.

"Didn't the sprinklers go off?" Ryan asked.

"Strangely, no," Edith said.

Scott stumbled out of the building assisting a young woman.

"My daughter? Did you see my daughter?" a man in his thirties asked Scott.

"No, not yet." Scott helped the woman to a nearby bench.

"I've gotta go find her."

Ryan blocked the young father. "Sir, you need to stay back."

Spence put a calming hand on the man's shoulder. "What's your name?"

"Rich."

"Rich, fire crews will be here any minute," Spence said.

"I'll go back in." Scott burst into a round of coughing.

"You've inhaled enough smoke," Spence said. "Do we even know she's inside?"

"Edith," Ryan said. "Was a little girl in there?"

"Yes, she came to watch us bake pastries for tomorrow's breakfast buffet. I thought someone grabbed her on the way out." She glanced at coworkers who all shook their heads that they hadn't.

Spence kept a firm grip on the father's shoulder to prevent him from rushing into a burning building.

"Where did you last see her?" Ryan asked Edith.

"Near the dishwasher. The smoke was coming from the storage closet, where we keep the linens. I don't get it. There's nothing flammable in there."

"You stay here," Ryan said to Spence and the father.

Ryan covered his mouth with his jacket sleeve and rushed into the building.

Spence scanned the group outside. Guests clung to their loved ones as they watched and waited for news about the fire.

"I didn't see any flames," a thirtysomething redheaded man said.

"I hope it wasn't Tina smoking a cigarette in the closet," a teenager said.

"I thought she quit," the redheaded man said.

"Who's Tina?" Spence asked.

"Our new assistant baker. Single mother of three," Edith offered. "Has anyone seen her?"

They all shook their heads that she didn't exit the building with them.

Spence eyed the smoke-filled hallway. Ryan was looking for a little girl near the dishwasher, but didn't know about the single mother who'd possibly been smoking in the closet.

Sirens echoed from the highway. They were still too far away. If Tina had accidentally set the fire…

Spence gripped the dad's shoulders and looked him in the eyes. "Rich, I'm putting you in charge. Make sure everyone stays clear of the building. That includes you. And assist the fire department when they arrive."

The father nodded. "Okay."

Spence turned and raced into the building.

He thought he heard someone shout his name from behind, but didn't let it distract him. He had to get inside; he had to help.

Shoving his jacket sleeve against his mouth, he slogged his way through the dense smoke. He stumbled down the hallway, wondering why the sprinklers hadn't gone off. He flung open the kitchen door.

"Ryan, it's Spence! Where are you?"

"I've got the girl!" Ryan said.

"There's another woman in here!"

"I've got her, too! Get outta here!"

Something snapped around his neck and yanked him back. Spence dug his fingers between his neck and what felt like braided rope.

The pressure cut off his airway. Someone shoved a cloth over his mouth, making it even harder to breathe.

"Don't fight it."

The rope loosened and he gasped for air, inhaling whatever was in the cloth.

The alarm grew distorted, sounding like the wail of an animal caught in a trap.

"Relax. It's almost over," the voice whispered.

SEVEN

"Spence!" Maddie called, pacing outside the door to the resort.

She couldn't believe he raced into a smoke-filled hallway. What was he thinking? He wasn't wearing equipment to protect him against fire. Was he that desperate to save lives?

Or was this bad judgment due to the brain injury?

And where was Ryan? He was supposed to be watching Spence, keeping him from doing anything foolish like rushing into a burning building.

Unless Ryan was also inside.

It took every ounce of self-control not to sprint into the resort after Spence, and possibly her brother, but common sense dictated she hang back.

Emergency vehicles finally pulled up. Vivian and her partner, Karl, pushed a stretcher toward the resort. Maddie spotted Sam Treadwell climb off Engine 52.

"Sam!" she called as he approached in full gear. "I saw Dr. Spencer run inside, and my brother might be in there, as well."

"Without gear?" he said, frustrated.

"Find them, please find them."

Sam motioned to his team. As they started for the door, it swung open and Ryan came out, holding a little girl in his arms. A young woman clung to Ryan's shoulder.

"Ryan!" Maddie cried rushing to her brother. He handed

the little girl to paramedics, and Maddie threw her arms around him.

"Anyone else inside?" Sam asked.

"I don't think so."

Maddie broke the hug. "Spence, where's Spence?"

"I told him to get out." Ryan scanned the area. "I thought he was ahead of me."

"We got this," Sam said. He and his team entered the resort.

"Are you okay?" Maddie asked her brother.

"Yeah."

She hugged him again and he said, "Hey, it's okay. Now you know how I felt when you didn't answer my call earlier." It wasn't a shaming comment, it was a caring one.

"I'm sorry about that," she said.

"I know, I know."

She broke the hug. "I'm worried about Spence."

"He called out to me. He was fine."

"He's still in there?" As Maddie glanced toward the resort, she realized the terrified, thirtysomething woman with brown hair clung to Ryan's shoulder.

Maddie nodded at her brother. "Have the medics examine her."

Ryan turned to the woman. "Ma'am, let's get you checked out."

She didn't respond, just stared at her hand that gripped his jacket.

"Come on, you're okay," he said, leading her to the ambulance.

Maddie took a few steps closer to the door, hoping to get a better look, hoping to see the guys from Engine 52 escorting Spence out of the building.

The alarm suddenly clicked off, blanketing the grounds in an eerie silence. She felt someone touch her shoulder. She glanced into her cousin Bree's eyes.

"Spence is still inside," Maddie said.

"The firemen will get him out."

Maddie nodded. A second ambulance pulled up to the side entrance. They were obviously prepared for multiple injuries.

Her cousin Aiden rushed toward them.

"You okay?" Nia asked.

"Of course I'm not okay. My resort's on fire." He glanced at Nia. "Sorry, hon." He kissed the top of her head. "How did this start?"

"We're not sure," Nia said. "Smoke suddenly filled the hallways from the kitchen area."

"Dr. Spencer is in there," Maddie said.

"Spence? Why?" Aiden asked, worried about his friend.

Maddie stared at the building. "I guess he needed to help."

"I should've gotten here sooner," Aiden said. He took a step toward the resort.

Nia blocked him. "Don't even think about it."

"Here comes Sam," Maddie said. The firefighter and his team came out of the building assisting two more people, but not Spence.

Maddie's heart sank. Before she could ask the firefighter about Spence, he spoke to the group.

"Everyone, you can go back to your rooms. It wasn't a fire, just a lotta smoke contained in the kitchen." Sam approached Aiden. "You've got a prankster on your hands. Someone set off a smoke bomb."

"Did you see Dr. Spencer?" Maddie asked.

"I saw county paramedics wheeling him away from the side exit," Sam said.

Maddie nodded. She didn't like that county had taken Spence because she didn't know those paramedics and couldn't push them for information about his condition.

As everyone started talking around her—Aiden barking orders, Sam speculating on the damage and the kitchen staff asking if they should go back inside and finish the baking— Maddie glanced beyond Aiden and spotted two men wheeling Spence toward an ambulance. The hair on the back of her neck pricked.

"Maddie?" Bree asked.

"How's Tina?" Aiden asked Ryan.

"She's okay. Relieved she didn't start the fire."

"Sam says it was some kind of smoke bomb," Aiden added.

"Kids?" Ryan said.

"Maddie, what is it?" Bree gripped Maddie's arm.

Maddie couldn't take her eyes off Spence being loaded into the ambulance.

Something felt off, but she wasn't sure what. Maybe she just needed to see for herself that he was okay. Or maybe it was something else…

"Maddie!" Ryan called out.

That's when she realized she was running toward the ambulance.

Follow your gut.

Bree had driven that message home over and over again to everyone in the McBride clan. As Maddie tore across the property, the ambulance sped off through a fog of smoke.

And there, on the ground, was a body.

"Spence," she gasped.

"Maddie!" Ryan caught up to her. "What are you—?"

He must have seen the body, as well.

She redirected her attention from the vanishing ambulance to the body, trying to calm her frantic heartbeat. Maybe it was someone from the fire who'd wandered out and collapsed.

Maybe it wasn't Spence.

She dropped to the ground and realized it wasn't Spence, but a paramedic. A gasp-choke escaped her lips.

The young paramedic sat up, rubbing his head.

"What happened?" Ryan said.

"We found an unconscious male by the south exit. Secured him in the back of the ambulance but when I opened the driver's door someone clobbered me."

Maddie snapped her attention into the fog, where the ambulance had vanished. "They took him, Ryan. They took Spence."

Spence opened his eyes, cataloging his surroundings. How had he ended up in an ambulance? He didn't think he'd inhaled that much smoke, but must have because he felt nauseous and disoriented. With the oxygen mask firmly over his face, Spence struggled to communicate with the male paramedic.

"Just relax," the young man said. "I'm Tyler, and my partner Eddie is driving."

Spence didn't know Tyler, which didn't help ease the tension in his chest. If only Maddie had been on duty and called to the scene.

Maddie. The sound of her shouting his name echoed in his mind. She *had* been there.

The ambulance jerked left and Tyler flew out of sight.

"Eddie, slow down!" Tyler shouted. He shifted back to the bench beside Spence and knocked on the window between them and the driver. "What's wrong with you?" Tyler shook his head and glanced at Spence. "Sorry about that. Eddie just broke up with his girlfriend."

Spence knew the pain of heartbreak; the memory of finding Andrea in the arms of another man still cut him to the quick. He surely must have inhaled too much smoke to be thinking about that disaster. He'd put that painful memory behind him, buried it deep where it could no longer hurt him.

The siren clicked on and the ambulance sped up.

"Eddie! It's mild smoke inhalation!" Tyler shook his head. "He's a good driver, don't worry." Tyler took Spence's blood pressure.

Spence removed his mask. "I don't know you."

"I'm Tyler, remember?"

"I've never seen you at the hospital. I'm…a doctor."

"I usually work in Skagit County, but they called us in on the resort fire." He adjusted the oxygen mask over Spence's mouth. "Please keep this on."

"Ambulance 112, this is base. Over." A voice said through Tyler's shoulder radio.

"This is Ambulance 112. Over," he responded.

"What's your twenty? Over."

Tyler knocked on the divider. "Eddie! They want our twenty!"

No response.

He knocked again. "Eddie!"

The ambulance swerved. Tyler jerked back, slamming into a cabinet. Gripping his head, he shouted, "That's enough! I'm driving!"

He pounded on the divider with his fist.

In Spence's eyes it seemed like everything was moving in slow motion. Had he inhaled more smoke than he thought?

Breathe, he coached himself. *Keep breathing.*

The ambulance pulled over.

"Hang tight," Tyler said, and disappeared from view.

Spence wasn't sure how long Tyler was gone. In his condition he didn't have a clear sense of time.

"Kyle," a voice said. "Your brother needs you."

His brother?

"Bobby?" Spence croaked.

"Yes, Bobby needs you. Let's go." A man's face came into view, but he wore a surgical mask and thick, tinted glasses.

"Bobby's here?" Spence said as the doctor led him out of the ambulance.

"Yes. I tried to help, but he's asking for you."

"Bobby," Spence hushed.

The ground tilted beneath his feet, but the doctor with the tinted glasses kept him upright, guiding him into the woods.

"What happened?" Spence said.

"He fell, remember?"

Spence nodded. Yes, he remembered. They were playing superheroes and Spence dared Bobby to jump across a ravine like Batman.

The doctor led Spence up a trail, his legs weak and unsteady.

"You're the only one who can help him."

Spence forced himself to be strong, to make it to his brother.

To save him this time.

They approached an overlook. The doctor let go of Spence's arm and retreated into the forest.

"Where is he?" Spence said.

"Down there. Can't you see him?"

Spence peered down into the mass of nothingness. "I can't…"

"Kyle," a voice echoed. "Kyle, help me."

Spence squinted to see below, to see his brother, but was blinded by darkness.

"Bobby?" Spence called back.

"Don't let me die!"

"I'm coming, Bobby!" Spence dropped to his stomach to lower himself to the ledge where his brother lay injured.

This time would be different. He'd help Bobby.

He'd save him.

"I'm coming, Bobby!"

"Spence!" a woman shouted.

Was Maddie down there with his brother? Together, Spence and Maddie would save Bobby for sure.

He grabbed on to a tree root and let his feet dangle, just like before, only he knew what to do this time. He was a doctor.

He was about to let go when firm hands gripped his wrists.

"Pull!" a man ordered.

In a swift movement, Spence was up on the trail lying on his back. "No, I have to get to Bobby."

He struggled to get up, but someone restrained him.

"Shh, it's okay." A pair of brilliant green eyes looked down at him.

Maddie.

"Take it easy, Spence," she said.

"Bobby, Bobby needs me."

She shone a bright light in his eyes. "He's been drugged," she said to someone.

Spence realized Nate was holding him down. "You're okay, buddy. Just relax," Nate said.

"Not okay. Bobby's hurt."

"Who's Bobby?" Maddie asked Nate. He shook his head.

"My little brother," Spence said, fighting the restraint of strong hands pressed against his shoulders.

"We've gotta get him to the hospital," Maddie said.

And he was up, being led away from the ledge, away from his brother.

"No, Bobby, no!" The pain and grief of his brother's death rushed though him. "It's my fault. He's dead because of me."

Maddie and Nate didn't want the Echo Mountain Hospital staff to witness Spence in such a disoriented state, so they took him to Cedar River, a hospital one county over. Nate had a friend there and made a call, asking if they could treat Spence quietly, without drawing unnecessary attention.

They loaded Spence into the county ambulance. Maddie stayed in the back with him and Ryan drove the ambulance to the hospital. The other paramedic, Tyler, had sustained a head injury and rode in front.

"It's my fault. Bobby... I killed my little brother," Spence whispered.

"No, you didn't kill anyone," Maddie said.

His eyes popped open. "Didn't you hear him? He was calling my name."

"Shh," Maddie said, stroking his soft, ash-blond hair. "Spence, look at me."

He blinked and looked into her eyes. "My brother…"

"It's okay. Everything's going to be okay." She didn't know what else to say.

"Bobby…" Spence closed his eyes.

This situation was growing worse instead of better. The perpetrator had assaulted not one, but two paramedics, kidnapped the doctor and tried to make him climb down a mountain. And how had he done that? By messing with Spence's mind. Which meant the attacker knew details about Spence's life. It was time Maddie knew the same details.

They pulled up to the hospital and Maddie opened the ambulance doors.

"Maddie," Spence said.

"I'm here."

Nate walked up to her. "They're letting us come in through the side entrance."

"Thanks. It would help if we knew what happened to Spence's brother."

"Detective Vaughn is working on it."

An ER doctor and nurse came out of the building. "I'm Dr. Reece. We'll take it from here."

"I need to stay with him," Maddie said. "He's disoriented and argumentative. My presence will keep him calm."

"This way."

Maddie and Nate followed them into the hospital, Maddie even more determined than ever to stay close to Spence.

A few hours later Maddie sat beside Spence's bed in the ER, waiting for results from a drug test. He'd been drugged, no question in her mind. Otherwise he wouldn't have been so out of it, and he surely wouldn't have tried to rappel down a mountainside at night with no equipment.

To get to Bobby, his little brother, who wasn't even there.

Her phone rang and she recognized her aunt's number. "Hey, Aunt Margaret."

"I heard about the fire at the resort. Is Dr. Spencer okay?"

"He will be."

"I had tea with Iris Price and she told me Anthony and Theresa are doing just fine. Set a wedding date for September."

"That's good news."

"Tell Dr. Spencer I'm making two more casseroles and a fruit plate for him."

"I'm sure he'll appreciate it."

"How about you? Are you okay?"

"Yes, ma'am. I'm good."

"Keep in touch, okay? Even if it's an email, but not text, I haven't figured out the texting thing yet."

"Sounds good. Love you."

The curtain pulled back and Nate motioned her to join him, away from Spence.

"I can't leave him," she said.

"I've got you covered." Nate motioned to a man standing a few feet away. "This is bodyguard Adam Swift. He owns a personal security firm and is going to keep an eye on Spence for us."

"Ma'am," Adam said in greeting.

In his thirties, he had short brown hair, a square jaw and wore a serious expression.

"How do we know we can trust him, Nate?" she asked. "No offense, Adam, but we've had a couple of crazy days."

"We served in the military together," Nate said. "He's solid and his is one of the top-rated agencies in the Seattle area."

With a nod, she followed Nate out of the ER into the lobby, leaving Adam to keep watch over Spence.

Nate led her to a secluded corner. "Spence had a brother named Robert who passed away at eight years old. Spence was thirteen. The report indicates that Spence and his brother were playing in a forest and Bobby fell. He sustained life-threatening injuries and died."

She glanced toward the ER examining area. "That's horrible."

"It sounds like Spence blames himself."

"But he was just a kid."

"You don't have to convince me. All that guilt must have come rushing back tonight."

"Because the kidnapper who assaulted the paramedics and drugged Spence shoved his failures in his face."

"Which means the kidnapper knows about his past."

"Yes, I figured that out, too." She crossed her arms over her chest. "Why is all this happening now? What triggered the attempts on his life?"

"Perhaps the answer is in your list of suspects."

"You got my email, right?"

"I did."

"Did you check out Dr. Danner's whereabouts during the time Gwen went searching for her phone?"

"Still working on that. Hard to believe professional jealousy could be behind this."

"You don't know Danner," she said wryly.

He glanced across the lobby. "I thought I knew Spence."

"Grief isn't something easily shared, especially when guilt is attached."

"True. Do you need a lift back to Echo Mountain Resort or will you be staying here?"

"I'm staying."

"Adam is a good man. He can protect him."

"Yes, but Adam a stranger. Spence needs to see a familiar face when he wakes up."

"Sounds good. I'd better get back. Adam can drive you and Spence to the resort when he's released. Keep me posted on his condition."

"Of course."

As Maddie headed to the ER examining area, she decided to find someone to cover her shift starting tomorrow at three. She didn't want to be away from Spence for a full twenty-four hours.

She called Vivian, but it went into voice mail so she left a message. "Hey, Vivian, it's Maddie. I'm in a pinch and need to get my shift covered, or at least part of it. It starts at three tomorrow afternoon. Let me know either way, okay? Thanks."

Maddie considered calling Wiggy Wunderman but knew Rocky would not be happy with her if he got stuck with the guy's nonstop chatter for a twenty-four-hour shift.

Suddenly a code blue echoed across the hospital PA system. Dr. Reece and a nurse rushed past Maddie into the ER exam area.

Where she'd left Spence.

Her heart slammed against her chest as she raced to the door and pushed it open.

"What's going on?" she said.

Adam blocked her.

"Get me the crash cart!" Dr. Reece shouted.

The words sent a chill down Maddie's spine.

EIGHT

The room seemed to close in. They needed a crash cart for Spence?

"Come on," Adam said, escorting Maddie out of the examining area.

Once in the lobby, she turned to him. "But I need to… you need to…someone needs to stay with him in case…in case…"

"Let the doctors do their job."

She snapped her attention to him. "I'm worried about someone coming after him again. Guard the door, don't let anyone in without an ID badge."

"You'll stay here?"

She nodded but couldn't speak, a knot of fear tangling her vocal cords. Adam crossed the lobby and stood guard beside the door.

Nate rushed up to Maddie. "I was almost outside and heard the code. It isn't—"

"Spence." She glanced at him, but didn't really focus.

Nate led her to the waiting area. "I don't understand."

"It must be the drugs." She glanced at Nate. "The only way this could happen is if the attacker gave him a drug that slowed down his heart or affected his breathing." She fisted her hands to stop the trembling. "Which means the perp has medical knowledge."

"That narrows things down," Nate said.

Silence vibrated around them like a low-frequency hum of an air-conditioning unit. Her gaze drifted to the door to the examining area. She'd treated her share of trauma patients with heart issues, but Spence was a healthy, active man in his thirties. What drug had he been given that affected his breathing or made his blood pressure drop dangerously low? "We brought him here thinking he'd be safe, yet he's in there fighting for his life," Maddie said. "This has got to end, Chief."

She stood and paced the waiting area. Nervous energy, frustration and even rage were tearing her up inside.

"Detective Vaughn is investigating the names you sent over. So far, no word on Lucas Winfield's whereabouts, and Roger Grimes is still under investigation about the abuse allegations. Detective Vaughn contacted a detective friend in Portland to look into the Tomlin family."

"Well, apparently Anthony Price and Theresa are back together, so we can scratch him off the list of revenge seekers. It mystifies me that Spence would have an enemy angry enough to want him dead."

"Or punished for a perceived wrong." Nate glanced at his phone. "I've got to take this." Nate went outside.

Maddie willed the ER examining area doors to open, wanting the doctor to come out and tell her Spence was okay.

Spence had to be okay because she would not accept any other outcome. She took a deep breath and said a silent prayer.

Nate returned wearing a frown. How could this night get any worse?

"What?" she said.

"Dr. Danner didn't show up for his shift today."

Spence squinted against the bright sun shining through the window. He realized he was in a hospital, but it wasn't Echo Mountain Hospital. Panic gripped his chest. Had the brain injury caused him to pass out?

"There you are," Maddie said, approaching his bed.

"Where am I?"

"Cedar River Hospital."

He nodded, but didn't ask the next question burning in his mind. *How did I get here*?

"What's the last thing you remember?" Maddie said.

"A kitchen fire at the resort. I went inside to find a young woman and then, then I was in an ambulance. Why was I in an ambulance?"

"Some creep-O knocked out the driver and drove off with you in the back. He drugged you, assaulted the other paramedic and tried convincing you to throw yourself off the mountainside. Do you remember that last part?"

Spence closed his eyes. Bobby's voice, he'd heard Bobby's voice.

"My brother," was all he could say.

"Your kidnapper was messing with your head, big-time. We think the drug caused hallucinations and worse, your BP dropped so low they almost lost you last night."

He nodded. Took a deep breath. And felt her hand touch his shoulder.

"I'm sorry," she said. "About your brother."

She knew the truth. He let Bobby die.

"Did they find the man who kidnapped me?" he said, not able to make eye contact.

"Spence, look at me."

He glanced into her eyes.

"Your brother's death was not your fault."

"You don't know anything about it," he snapped. "You weren't there."

"No, I wasn't. But I know a thirteen-year-old boy shouldn't be held responsible for an accident. Is that why you went into medicine?"

He nodded.

"It's a blessing you did. Think of all the people you've helped as a doctor."

"It'll never be enough," he said. "I didn't help the one who mattered most."

"If Bobby were here right now, do you think he'd want you be punishing yourself like this?"

He glared at her. "He's not here. That's the point. And what are you, my counselor?"

An expression he'd never seen before flashed in her green eyes. His words had hurt her, deeply. Probably a good thing. He had wanted to drive her away, and perhaps this would finally do it.

She slipped her hand off his shoulder and went to the window. He suddenly wanted to apologize. He wasn't a cruel man and the thought of intentionally hurting her flooded him with guilt.

Worse, she knew his biggest shame, the one thing that drove his every thought: he was a failure who let down the people he loved most. What else would explain Andrea falling for another man? Because Spence hadn't been loving enough, caring enough.

Good enough.

His failures started long before that. After his brother's death he'd never been able to recapture his parents' love. No matter what he did or how hard he tried, he continually let them down.

Maddie's phone vibrated and she pulled it out of her pocket. "I'll be right back," she said, walking past him without looking up.

She disappeared into the hallway leaving him alone with his thoughts and despair. It always seemed less painful when she was nearby talking to him, forgiving him.

But she deserved a better man than a damaged doctor with emotionally paralyzing scars of shame.

Being in the hospital wasn't helping the situation, especially since Dr. Carver would eventually hear he'd been admitted again, delaying his return to the schedule. She had questioned his decision to return to work the other day.

FREE Merchandise is 'in the Cards' for you!

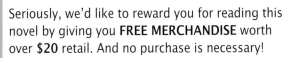

Dear Reader,

We're giving away FREE MERCHANDISE!

Seriously, we'd like to reward you for reading this novel by giving you **FREE MERCHANDISE** worth over $20 retail. And no purchase is necessary!

You see the Jack of Hearts sticker above? Paste that sticker in the box on the Free Merchandise Voucher inside. Return the Voucher today… and we'll send you Free Merchandise!

Thanks again for reading one of our novels—and enjoy your Free Merchandise with our compliments!

Pam Powers

Pam Powers

P.S. Look inside to see what Free Merchandise is **"in the cards"** for you!

W
e'd like to send you two free books like the one you are enjoying now. Your two books have a combined price of over $10 retail, but they are yours to keep absolutely FREE! We'll even send you 2 wonderful surprise gifts. You can't lose!

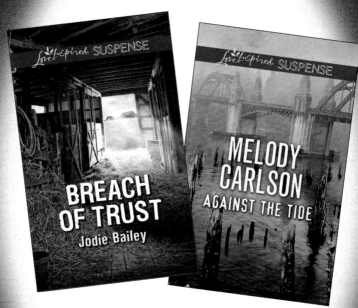

REMEMBER: Your Free Merchandise, consisting of **2 Free Books** and **2 Free Gifts**, is worth over $20 retail! No purchase is necessary, so please send for your Free Merchandise today.

Get TWO FREE GIFTS!

We'll also send you 2 wonderful FREE GIFTS (worth about $10 retail), in addition to your 2 Free books!

Visit us at:
www.ReaderService.com

Books received may not be as shown.

What would she think when she heard he'd hallucinated his brother's accident?

The longer he stayed here the worse it was for his career, his life.

He shifted out of bed, letting his bare feet touch the cool vinyl floor. He seemed steady enough. Taking a few steps, his head grew light, but he forged on.

"Whoa, whoa," Maddie said, coming into the room and gripping his arm for support. "What are you trying to do?"

"I'm leaving."

"You sure that's a good idea? You coded last night."

"Because of a drug reaction. I suppose you think I should spend another night in the hospital?"

She crossed her arms over her chest, but didn't answer.

"I get it, now you're not talking to me," he said.

"Why should I? I only seem to make you angry with your snappy comments and insults. And ya know, I don't deserve that. All I've done is try to help you stay alive. So you're welcome and goodbye." She turned to leave.

Spence gently grabbed her wrist. "Wait."

She turned to him with fire in her eyes.

"You know what they say about people being the hardest on those closest to them?" he said.

Clenching her jaw, she nodded.

"In the past few days I've become closer and more comfortable with you than anyone else in my circle of friends," he said. "What I'm trying to say is, I'm lashing out because, on some level, I know that you'll forgive me. But that's not the only reason."

The clench of her jaw softened.

"Maddie, the thought of something happening to you because of my problems…" He hesitated before continuing, "Well, it makes me crazy, and I lash out. It's no excuse for my behavior and I am sorry. To be blunt, I don't have much experience with this type of relationship."

Spence released her wrist. He said his piece and figured

she'd leave. Instead, she narrowed her eyes as if assessing his confession.

Finally she said, "Nate hired you a bodyguard. His name is Adam and he'll take us back to the resort."

That's it? Spence thought. He'd bared his soul to her, admitted that he felt closer to her than anyone else in his life, and all she could say was a bodyguard would take them back to Echo Mountain?

His heart sank. The damage was done. He'd successfully driven her away and should be happy.

"Do you need help getting dressed? I can get a nurse," she said.

"No, I'll manage."

With a nod, she left the hospital room.

As the bodyguard drove them back to the resort in his SUV, Spence's words taunted Maddie.

I'm lashing out because, on some level, I know that you'll forgive me.

Had that been her problem all along? That her ability to forgive was actually a weakness that made people take advantage of her?

No, she wouldn't believe that. Her faith had taught her the importance of forgiveness and love, two things that always opened the door to grace.

Sure, she'd suffered painful relationships, but that shouldn't affect her desire to forgive others. She was strong in her faith, so something else was niggling at her thoughts on the drive back to Echo Mountain.

I don't have much experience with this type of relationship.

What kind of relationship? She wasn't sure. It was indefinable in the traditional sense. She knew private things about Spence that he'd worked so hard to keep hidden, like how his brain injury had affected his abilities after the attack, and how he blamed himself for his brother's death. He wanted to keep these things a secret, yet needed to lean on someone, trust someone.

Maddie had shown up at the right moment in the forest, and had the necessary skills to both save his life and become a confidant.

What would happen when the mystery was solved and the perpetrator was charged and locked up? Would there be a relationship between her and Spence then?

Probably not. Her goal in life was to stay grounded and fight, not run from challenges. She wondered if Spence ran from his Portland position because of his patient's death. Starting a new life with a clean slate was great in theory, but it seemed to Maddie that you brought all of your emotional baggage with you, so who's to say you wouldn't recreate the same situation in a new town?

No, Maddie wasn't running away like her parents or Waylan. She enjoyed helping people through her work as a paramedic, and volunteering at church and the homeless shelter.

Spence, on the other hand, was a professional who could land a job anywhere, and would probably head back to a big city where he belonged.

You'd better guard your heart before it gets broken, she warned herself.

"Do you want me to drop you off somewhere?" Adam the bodyguard asked, eyeing her through the rearview mirror.

"No, I'll go back to the resort with Dr. Spencer." She glanced at Spence, whose eyes were closed. "Unless you'd rather I not come back with you?"

He didn't answer.

"Spence?"

He glanced at her. "Sorry, what?"

"I'm going to the resort with you, unless you'd rather I not."

"I—" he stuttered, "I wouldn't mind the company, if you can work it into your schedule."

She shot him a look. Wouldn't mind the company?

"I guess that sounded less than enthusiastic," he said. "I feel guilty about taking you away from your life."

She glanced at Adam. "I'll go to the resort. Can we swing by my apartment first?"

"Sure."

She gave him the address and turned back to Spence. He'd closed his eyes again.

She touched his arm. "You okay?"

"Still tired from whatever drug they gave me yesterday."

"Rest is probably the best thing."

They'd stopped by her place, she'd packed a bag and they headed for the resort. Aiden greeted them with a key to a new cabin. Nate suggested they relocate in case the assailant had seen which cabin Spence had come from last night. The general assumption was that the assailant set off the smoke device in order to draw Spence out of hiding.

Maddie and Adam were helping Spence settle into the new cabin when she finally got a callback about shift coverage. She'd made a lot of calls that morning, trying to find a sub.

"Hey, Vivian," Maddie answered. "Thanks for calling back."

"Yeah, so I'd love to take your shift, but I'm in the city and won't get back until eight. I could cover you from around nine tonight through the end of your shift tomorrow, or is that too weird?"

"No, that would be great." Maddie was pleased that she found the partial shift coverage. "Text me when you're ready to take over and we'll swing by your place to pick you up."

"Sounds good. Is Rocky on tonight?"

Maddie suspected Vivian had a crush on Maddie's friend. "He is."

"Cool. Okay, then talk to you later."

Maddie smiled. Maybe there was hope for Rocky's love life after all. She joined Spence in the living area where he was leaning back in a thick-cushioned chair, his brows furrowed.

"What's bothering you?" she said.

"They still haven't found Dr. Danner."

"Yeah, that's weird. I mean, how is he involved in all this?"

Spence shook his head.

"Where's your bodyguard?" she asked.

"Adam is outside checking the grounds for—" he made quotes with his fingers "—vulnerabilities."

"He seems professional. Well, I was able to get most of my shift covered."

"I don't think that's a good idea."

"What, taking time off?"

"Going out in public. You're safer here, with me and Adam, or at Bree's or even your Aunt Margaret's farm."

"Whoa, slow down. I'm not the one they're after, remember?"

"You're a part of this now, Maddie."

"I'll be safe at the firehouse. Chances are we won't even be called out during the first six hours of the shift. Besides, the cops in town have the sketch of the bearded guy so they'll be on the lookout."

"I think you should call Nate."

"I'm sure he has more important things on his plate." She could tell Spence was worried. "Okay, I'll let him know I'll be on shift from three to nine."

"Good." He stood and walked to the kitchen counter. "I've decided it's time for me to stop being so passive."

"Passive? You've been injured multiple times. That's not being passive."

"Regardless, I'm done being terrorized. And now they've got Dr. Danner?"

"We don't know that for sure."

"I need to put a stop to this, protect myself, and you."

"You're still recovering. Maybe you should take it easy."

"I'm done taking it easy." He pointed to the whiteboard. "I'm going to check people off the list one by one. I'll contact Theresa—"

"Not necessary. My aunt told me Anthony and Theresa have set a wedding date."

"Good, how about—?"

"Nate's on it. He told me at the hospital that Roger Grimes is still under investigation and there's no word about Lucas's whereabouts. Hey, I've got an idea."

"Skip work?"

"I'll be fine. So Roger Grimes is an insurance salesman, right?" she said.

"How do you know that?"

"He stopped by the firehouse to see if any of us needed life insurance. I could call him and act like I'm interested, then get him talking to get a sense of his state of mind."

"No, it's too dangerous."

"We could meet at a coffee shop. I'll have my brother sitting in the corner keeping watch."

"I feel like we'd do better by starting at the beginning, with Gwen."

"You mean visit her in the hospital?" Maddie asked.

"Yes."

"What's she going to tell you that she hasn't told Nate?"

"She trusts me." He turned to her, his blue eyes reflecting a kind of raw emotion she'd never seen before. "Like I've grown to trust you."

She wasn't sure what to say.

I don't have much experience with this type of relationship.

She was about to ask him to define their relationship so she could be on the same page, when he said, "I'm sorry if that was too forward. I haven't felt this kind of close connection to someone in a very long time."

She struggled to process her own feelings, wanting desperately to keep things professional. "I'm glad I could be there for you."

* * *

Maddie started her shift at three and by seven o'clock it looked like it was going to be a quiet evening, as she'd predicted. Sitting in the lounge at the fire station, she was reading the local paper when she came across a story about a burglary at the Winfield home.

She sat up straight. The house had been trashed, and nothing expensive had been taken, mostly food, supplies and flashlights. Stories like these sparked fear in local residents, fear that a homeless person had become desperate enough to commit a crime.

There was a homeless encampment north of town, close to a bus stop that allowed the residents to commute to work either in Echo Mountain or surrounding communities. The homeless residents Maddie had met while volunteering were good people that had fallen on hard times and needed temporary help.

As she studied the newspaper, she had another thought: Lucas could have come home and taken what he needed to survive on his own.

She pulled out her phone to share her observation with Spence. Rocky flopped down next to her.

"Thanks," he said.

"For what?" She pocketed her phone.

"Not sticking me with Wiggy."

"You're welcome. I thought you were out getting dinner."

"Let's take a drive and pick up some burgers."

She considered, wanting to keep her word to Spence about staying at the firehouse if not on a call.

"What? You want Chinese instead?" Rocky said.

"No, burgers are fine."

They got into the ambulance and headed out. Any emergency calls would be patched through to their vehicle.

"Did you hear Dr. Danner didn't show up for his shift today?" Rocky said.

"I did hear that."

"Being that you're so close to Dr. Perfect you probably know more scoop than any of us."

"We're not that close."

"Uh-huh. So what do you think happened to Danner? Went fishing and got eaten by a salmon? Got lost on a nature walk?"

"Very funny. Actually I'm wondering if he's behind the attacks on Spence and has fled the state."

"Spence?" Rocky shot her a side glance. "I thought you weren't that close."

"He wants me to call him Spence. What's the big deal?"

Rocky shook his head. "You can be so naive sometimes."

"Ambulance 64, please respond to an injured party at 890 Industrial Drive. Over."

Maddie grabbed the radio. "Ten-four, base."

Rocky flipped on the siren and they sped off. A few minutes later they pulled up to an office building under construction. It had only partial outer walls, and looked downright creepy at night.

"I didn't know these crews worked past five," she said.

"Probably kids messing around and someone got hurt."

They grabbed the equipment and headed to the stairs. "Dispatch, did they give a floor number? Over." Rocky asked.

"Fifth floor. Over."

"Service elevator?" she asked Rocky.

"I need my exercise." Rocky winked, heading for the stairs.

Maddie appreciated Rocky's lighthearted nature at times like this. It was important to balance the stress with humor when heading into a tense situation. They made it to the fifth floor.

"Echo Mountain Emergency!" Rocky called out.

A crack whistled through the air.

NINE

Maddie instinctively grabbed Rocky and pulled him to the floor.

Another crack rang out, and only then did she accept what was happening. She called in on her radio. "Dispatch, someone's shooting at us. Send help! Over!"

"Officer Carrington is on the way. Over."

"Fifth floor, tell him we're on the fifth floor. Over," Maddie said. "Red's on the way," she said to her partner.

When Rocky didn't answer she glanced at him. A blood-stain spread across his jacket.

"No, no, no," she muttered, grabbing gauze out of her bag.

"My partner's been hit," she said into her radio.

Rocky groaned and opened his eyes. "What's happening?"

"Someone's shooting at us."

"Get out of here. Go!" he ordered.

Another shot pierced the night air. Heart pounding, she knew there was no way she could leave her friend.

She also knew she might die tonight.

Without having spoken her truth to Spence.

She should have told him she'd felt it, too, an unusually close connection that scared the wits out of her because in her experience that kind of emotion was usually followed by pain.

"Man, that stings," Rocky said.

She put more pressure on his shoulder wound to stop the bleeding. "You'll be okay."

"I'll be better once you're safe."

"I'm waiting for the police." She glanced nervously over her shoulder.

"Why is he using us as target practice if we're here to help him?"

"Unless it was a trap."

"A trap?" Rocky sat up and winced.

"It might have something to do with Dr. Spencer."

He snapped his attention to her. "What are you talking about?"

"Spence didn't want me to go on shift tonight. He thought it might be dangerous, but I said I'd most likely be at the station and ignored his concern…and now, now you've been shot, because of me."

"Knock it off. None of this is your fault."

She couldn't make eye contact, ashamed that she'd put his life in danger because she hadn't taken Spence's warning seriously.

"Hey, look at me."

She slowly turned to her friend.

"Did you shoot me in the shoulder?"

"No, but—"

"No. This isn't your fault."

"Maddie McBride!" a man called out.

Rocky touched her arm. "Don't."

"What do you want?" she shouted back.

"Tell me where Dr. Spencer is and I won't hurt you."

"Are you kidding me? You shot my partner! Police are on the way!"

"They won't get here in time." His voice seemed closer.

Her pulse raced. They had to get out of here. She gripped Rocky's uninjured arm and whispered, "Let's move."

With a nod, Rocky stood. She shouldered the medical supplies bag and they stayed low.

"It's a simple question!" the assailant yelled.

And if she gave the answer, Spence would be assaulted again, plus the shooter would have no reason to keep her and Rocky alive.

"Ambulance 64," dispatch called over the radio. She turned down the volume so it wouldn't make them easy targets. Then she realized the shooter probably figured they would head for the service elevator.

"Stairs," she whispered to Rocky. She hoped he could manage the stairs in his condition.

With his uninjured arm around her shoulder, they passed the elevator and turned a corner.

Another shot rang out.

Maddie pulled Rocky down again.

She heard the stairwell door swing open a few feet away.

Two more shots were fired.

She held her breath. Prayed.

"Are you hurt?" It was her brother's voice.

She snapped her eyes open and saw him standing over her, his gaze focused beyond them.

"I'm okay," she said.

Officer Carrington burst through the stairwell door, gun drawn.

"That way." Ryan motioned and crouched beside Maddie.

Red took off in pursuit of the shooter.

"Ryan? I… I…" Her voice caught in her throat.

"You did good, sis." Ryan kept his hand on his firearm and his gaze focused in the direction of the shooter.

"Did you hit him?" she asked.

"Not sure. How's Rocky?"

"A little bloody, but I'll live," Rocky said. "You guys got here fast."

"Dr. Spencer called the chief, worried about Maddie being on shift tonight, so I've been monitoring your calls. Got here as soon as I could."

"Stop! Police!" Red's voice echoed.

More shots rang out and she automatically ducked. A few seconds later, her brother squeezed her shoulder. She glanced up as Red approached them. "I think you hit him," Red said to Ryan. "He was limping to his car down below. He took off in a small SUV. I'll call in the description." Red spoke into his radio.

Maddie suddenly realized her brother was not in uniform. "Wait, you're off duty."

He smiled. "Never off duty for family."

A sense of dread awakened Spence. He shouldn't have napped after dinner, but his sleep schedule was off because of the drug working its way through his system.

Well, that and the constant worry that Maddie was in trouble.

He went into the living room and was greeted by Adam, who sat at the kitchen table. "Good nap?"

"Sure, I guess." Spence eyed the microwave clock. It was nearly nine, which meant Maddie's sub would already be there to relieve her. Spence hoped Maddie would return to his cabin, at least to let him know she was okay. A text or phone call would satisfy some people, but he always felt better when he saw her in person.

A firm knock echoed across the cabin.

Adam went to answer it. "Stay out of sight, Doc."

Spence went into the kitchen where he couldn't be seen from the door.

"Yes?" Adam asked.

"It's Nate."

Adam let him inside and Spence stepped out of hiding. "I didn't expect you to see you tonight unless… What happened?"

"Adam, can you give us a few minutes?"

"Sure." With a nod, Adam left, shutting the door with a click.

"What is it?" Spence pressed.

"Let's sit down."

"Tell me she's okay."

"She's okay."

Relieved, Spence went to the sofa and collapsed. Nate sat in a chair on the other side of the coffee table.

"They got a false call and someone was waiting," Nate said.

"The guy from the mountains?"

"We don't know for sure."

"What happened? Did he hurt her?" Spence fisted his hand.

"He fired at them—"

"But she's okay?"

"Yes."

"That's why I told her not to go to work. I was afraid something like this would happen because of this mess I'm in. And I'm ending it. I'm going down the checklist one by one and scratching off these so-called enemies before she gets seriously hurt."

"This is why I came by to talk to you, because I knew it would make you crazy."

"Of course I am. Wouldn't you be crazy if it was Cassie?"

Nate narrowed his eyes at Spence.

"You're sure she's not hurt?" Spence redirected.

"Not physically, but tonight will be hard to forget. Her partner, Rocky, was shot."

"Why? Why shoot at either of them?"

Nate glanced at the Echo Mountain PD hat he clutched between his fingers.

"Nate?"

"He wanted your location."

"Great, just great. Tell me you caught the guy."

"He got away, but was shot. I alerted the hospitals. It's just a matter of time before he shows up needing medical attention."

Spence leaned back against the sofa. "So, it's almost over."

"I'd like to think that, too, but…"

"But what?"

"You didn't recognize him when he broke into your cabin, right?"

"I'd never seen him before."

"I doubt a complete stranger would try to kill you multiple times, and shoot at two paramedics to get your location without a good motivation."

"Meaning what?"

"He was hired by someone."

"You're saying he's a hit man?"

"Yes, but not a very good one. I think he's an amateur, or small-time criminal, which means we'll catch him."

"Maddie and I will help expedite the process."

"No, I want you to take it easy."

"I can't. Not until I know Maddie is completely out of danger."

"Maddie? What about you?"

"If something happens to me, it happens. But if anything were to happen to Maddie…" His voice trailed off.

"Spence, this thing between you and Maddie—"

"I like her, Nate. A lot."

A knock was followed by Adam cracking open the door. "Someone wants to see you, Dr. Spencer."

Adam stepped aside and Maddie entered the cabin. Spence couldn't control the rush of relief at seeing her beautiful face. In three steps he crossed the room and held her in his arms. It felt so natural, like he'd been hugging her for most of his life.

Then he worried that the embrace was making her uncomfortable.

Breaking the hug, he looked into her eyes. "You're okay," is all he could say.

She nodded, and hugged him again.

* * *

The next morning Spence awoke with a sense of peace and his headache was finally gone. Maddie had spent an hour with him last night, relaxing in front of the fire. He encouraged her to talk about what had happened—the fear and the adrenaline rush of being shot at—to help her process the traumatic experience.

Then her brother showed up and escorted her across the resort compound to her cousin Bree's cottage. The cottage had a state-of-the-art alarm system and her brother would stay on the premises to keep watch, as well.

Although the assailant had been shot, they didn't know how seriously he'd been injured and feared he might continue his quest to come after Spence and Maddie.

Frustrated, Spence knew what he had to do: stop being a victim and take more aggressive action. He got dressed and opened his bedroom door, half-hoping he'd find Maddie sitting at the kitchen table. Instead, he was alone.

He spotted a note on the refrigerator from Adam explaining he was outside on the porch getting some air if Spence needed him.

What Spence needed was to feel better and put an end to this deadly drama.

He also needed Maddie.

He *needed* her? How had that happened?

Spence brewed tea and glanced out the kitchen window. The sun shone in such contrast to the murky dread hovering at the recesses of his brain.

Dread, frustration, helplessness.

Maybe he should have another MRI to see if the swelling had increased because these weren't typical feelings for Spence. He was generally content, as long as he was working.

Work withdrawal could be causing him to feel anxious, well that and the thought he'd almost lost Maddie. He clenched his jaw. She was an innocent in all this, responding to a SAR call in the mountains and saving his life. He couldn't thank her enough.

He wondered if he was so drawn to her because she took care of him without judgment or criticism, and graciously put up with his mood swings.

He remembered the look on his parents' faces after Bobby's death, their expression of disappointment and disgust. It followed him throughout his life.

The cabin door opened and he turned with a smile, hoping to see Maddie. Adam poked his head inside. "Bree wanted to drop off some food."

"Great, thanks, Adam," Spence said.

"I'm staying out here for a little while longer," Adam said.

Spence couldn't blame him. Being inside all the time was starting to drive Spence crazy.

Maddie's cousin Bree entered the cabin carrying a large bag.

"Thanks for the food, Bree," Spence said.

She slid it onto the counter. "Of course."

"How's Maddie?"

"You mean, where's Maddie?" She raised an eyebrow, opened the refrigerator and started loading it with food. "She's still asleep. Ryan will keep watch until I get back. I suspect she'll want to come over and share some of this food. Mom made most of it."

"I'm very grateful to your entire family."

She shut the refrigerator door. "Then how about doing something for us?"

"Sure, anything."

She folded her paper bag with delicate precision. "It's about Maddie."

"What about her?"

"This is going to sound corny but—" she sighed "—be careful with her. She seems tough but she's been hurt, a lot. And before you say anything about me misreading things—"

"I wasn't going to say that."

"So you admit there's something going on between you two?"

He glanced at the sofa where Maddie had leaned against his chest last night as they watched the fire.

"Yes, there's something," he said.

"I don't want this to sound disrespectful, I mean my brother thinks highly of you, as does the chief…"

"But?"

"I always got the feeling this was a temporary stop for you, that after a few years you'd move back to the city and a more prestigious medical practice. What I'm saying is, if you don't think you'll take this thing with Maddie to the end, then stop right now. Don't let her come over and take care of you. She's got such a big heart and she's been hurt by people who supposedly loved her."

"I would never intentionally hurt her."

"I'm sure you wouldn't, but I know my cousin. She'd do anything for someone she cared deeply about, even at her own expense."

Bree slipped the bag under her arm and started for the door. "Sorry if this conversation made you uncomfortable, but I'm protective of my cousin."

"I know the feeling."

"But was I right? About you wanting to move on after Echo Mountain?"

"It's a possibility, yes."

She turned to him. "That's too bad. I just don't see Maddie going anywhere. She loves her family and community too much to leave."

As she opened the door, Maddie and Ryan stepped onto the porch.

"What are you doing here?" Maddie said with a curious expression.

"Delivering food from Mom," Bree said. "I'd better get to work."

Maddie and Ryan came inside and joined Spence at the kitchen table.

"Any word on the guy who was shot last night?" Spence asked Ryan.

"He hasn't shown up in any area ERs yet, but we found the vehicle abandoned in a shopping center parking lot. It's registered to someone named Alex Moors. You know him?"

"The name is not familiar."

"Maybe he was a patient, either here or in Portland?" Maddie suggested.

"I'll look into it," Ryan said.

"Actually, let me," Spence offered. "I can make some calls to my former employer and determine if he was one of my patients."

"That'd be great." Ryan glanced at his sister. "Don't go anywhere alone. It's easier for us if you two stay together, under Adam's protection."

"Sounds good," Maddie said.

"Text if you need anything."

"I will. Thanks, Ryan." She hugged her brother and he left. She smiled at Spence, "So, you ready to get to work?"

"Oh yeah."

"What's first?"

"First, you tell me you slept okay."

"I'm famished." She went to the refrigerator.

"I'm sorry," he said, assuming she'd evaded the question because he wouldn't like the answer. "Did you sleep at all?"

"Here and there, and in between I'd pray."

"Pray?"

"I'd say prayers of gratitude that I wasn't hurt, that Rocky wasn't seriously hurt, that my brother wasn't shot by the creep, all that stuff."

She shut the refrigerator, holding a plastic container in her hand. "You ever have eggs baked in ham cups? They're yummy."

Bree's words taunted him. *If you don't think you'll take this thing with Maddie to the end, then stop right now.*

He should shut down the relationship brewing between them because he didn't know where his career would take him. He was a drifter, a nomad who didn't feel connected to any specific place, whereas Maddie belonged in Echo Mountain with her family.

"I've made a decision," he said.

Maddie slowly placed the container on the table. "That sounds serious."

"It's about us."

Maddie's eyes widened and she gripped the back of a chair as if bracing herself.

He struggled to form the words. It would start with an apology for all the violence he'd brought into her life. He opened his mouth, but nothing came out.

"Well, you're not down on one knee so you're not about to propose," she teased. "Let's see what else could it be?" She eyed the plastic container. "You hate ham cups?"

"I don't want you to get hurt."

"That makes two of us. Let's have breakfast."

"I should be telling you to leave."

"What, and miss my aunt's cooking?"

"You're teasing but I'm trying to be serious."

"I know, it's just…" She sighed. "There's so much serious stuff going on right now. Can't we just take it easy and enjoy a nice meal together?"

He sighed. "Sure."

After a hearty breakfast, Spence contacted the Portland hospital but there was no record of an Alex Moors having been treated there.

He decided to visit Gwen at the hospital and while he was there, inquire about Alex Moors. Perhaps if Ruth saw Spence fully functional, it would give her confidence that his condition was improving.

Maddie would go with him, and they'd keep Nate and her brother in the loop.

Spence was impressed by bodyguard Adam's ability to catalog each and every person in their immediate surroundings to assess danger. They made it to the hospital shortly after lunch. Maddie bought a colorful plant from the hospital gift shop for Gwen.

Since Spence had a relationship, make that a friendship, with Theresa in Billing, he decided to check with her to see if there was a patient record for Alex Moors.

Maddie waited outside the office. Spence wondered if she was uncomfortable because he'd told her that Theresa might have a crush on him. Or could Maddie be jealous?

"Hey, Theresa," Spence said, entering her office.

She glanced up from her computer screen with pleasant surprise. "Dr. Spencer." She stood to greet him. "I heard what happened. We were all so worried."

"I'm doing better thanks. I was wondering if you could do me a favor."

"Sure, anything."

"Can you check to see if there's ever been a patient at Echo Mountain Hospital named Alex Moors?"

"Of course. Who is he?" She tapped on her keyboard.

"We're not sure, possibly the man who's been threatening me."

Her fingers froze on the keyboard. She glanced up with concerned brown eyes. "I'm so sorry you're dealing with all this."

"Thanks. The sooner we figure out who's orchestrating the attacks, the sooner I can put it behind me."

She redirected her attention to the screen. "Let's see, Montlake... Muir. No Moors." She glanced up. "Sorry."

"Ah well, it was a long shot."

She came around to the front of her desk. "Be careful." She gave him a hug and he politely returned the gesture.

"Excuse me," a male voice said.

Theresa released Spence. A furious-looking Anthony stood inside the office clenching reddened fists by his sides. The man looked ready to explode.

"I'd appreciate it if you'd keep your hands off my fiancée," Anthony said.

"Cool it, Anthony," Theresa said, sitting behind her desk. "Dr. Spencer's been through a lot."

Spence nodded at Anthony. "Congratulations on your engagement. I heard you set a date."

The thirtysomething man glared at Spence.

"Ready, Dr. Spencer?" Maddie said from the doorway.

With a nod, Spence joined Maddie. Anthony shut the door behind them.

"Yikes, that was awkward," Maddie said.

"He's possessive."

"A control freak like that would drive me batty."

"At any rate, there's no record of an Alex Moors," Spence said.

"Huh, so he wasn't a patient," Maddie said.

"Doesn't look like it."

They approached Gwen's hospital room and Maddie touched his jacket sleeve. "You sure I should go in with you? Maybe she'd feel better talking to you alone."

"You helped save her life. I think she'd find comfort in seeing you." Spence motioned Maddie into the room. "Knock, knock."

Gwen's mother, Allison, helped her daughter sit up in bed.

"Dr. Spencer, hi," Gwen said.

Spence noted that her color looked much better than when he'd found her.

Maddie offered Gwen the colorful plant. "This is for you."

Gwen cast a wary glance at Maddie.

"Not sure if you remember Maddie McBride, but she helped me save your life up in the mountains," Spence said.

Her mom took the plant. "Gwen, what do you say?"

"Thanks."

Gwen's mom placed the plant on the window ledge next to half a dozen other arrangements. She turned back to Maddie and Spence. "I can't thank you enough for what you've done for Gwen."

"Of course," Maddie said.

"Do you think Gwen will be released soon, Doctor?" Allison asked.

"Actually, I'm off the rotation for a while," Spence said.

"Why?" Gwen asked, hugging her midsection.

"Recovering from brain trauma," he said, not wanting to share the other reason. "I'm sure Dr. Carver will release you as soon as she thinks it's appropriate. I was wondering if you'd be up to discussing what happened the other day in the mountains."

Gwen shrugged. "Sure, I guess."

"Is it okay with your mom?" Spence asked.

Allison nodded. "Of course."

"I heard you lost your phone and went looking for it by using an app," Spence started.

"Borrowed Mom's phone."

"Without my permission," Allison added.

"I said I was sorry."

"You're right, you did."

Gwen pouted for a second, then continued. "I hiked into the mountains, thinking I'd left it up there."

"So you've been to that location before?" Spence said.

"Me and my friends go up there sometimes to hang out."

"And smoke pot," her mom offered.

"Mom!" Gwen said.

Allison sighed. "I'm going to get a cup of coffee."

"I'll go with you," Maddie said.

The women left Gwen's room and she sighed. "Nothing I do makes her happy."

"She loves you. She's worried about you."

"Whatever."

Spence pulled up a chair. "So, you went looking for your phone," he prompted.

"The app said I found it, but all I saw was this guy lying on the ground. At first I thought he was hurt or something. I said, 'Hey, you okay?' He stood up and was wearing this creepy ski mask. I totally freaked and ran, but he caught me and threw me down. That's all I remember."

"That must have been terrifying. I'm sorry."

"I'm glad you were there. Why were you there, anyway?"

"I got a text from your phone asking for help."

"But I didn't have my phone."

"We'll let the police figure that part out."

She nodded, thoughtful. "I wonder if this has something to do with Wicker."

"Who?"

"A guy who hangs out with us, that's his nickname. He's older, in his twenties. He gets us pills sometimes."

"Did you give his name to Police Chief Walsh?"

She shook her head.

"Why not?"

"I don't want to get anyone in trouble."

"It's Wicker's choice to sell drugs to minors, not yours. If he's older he should know better, right?"

"I guess."

"Dr. Spencer?" a man said.

Spence turned to see Vince Brunson, board president, standing in the doorway. "Hi, Mr. Brunson."

"I thought you were on leave."

"I am, just checking on my favorite patient."

"I was under the impression you're in no condition to be treating patients."

"I'm not here in an official capacity."

Ruth brushed past Brunson and entered the room. "Spence," she said with surprise in her voice. "I didn't expect to see you."

"Dr. Carver, I'm not sure it's a good idea for a staff member with a brain injury—"

"As I said, this isn't an official visit," Spence interrupted. Brunson sighed, shook his head and left.

"What's his problem?" Spence muttered.

"You want the full list?" Ruth winked, then turned to Gwen. "How are you doing today?"

"Better. Throat's sore."

"From the tube. A good thing it wasn't a serious injury, and you could breathe on your own," Ruth said.

"When can I go home?" Gwen asked.

Ruth consulted her tablet. "Don't you like the food here?" she teased.

"Orange Jell-O has never been my favorite."

"What then, red or purple?" Ruth asked. "We don't want to discharge you too soon."

Gwen released a deep sigh.

"And after you're released I hope we don't see you back here anytime soon." Ruth winked.

"I think this experience has scared Gwen enough to stay out of trouble until she goes to college next fall," Spence said.

"If I get into college," she muttered.

"I can help with that," Spence said. "I aced my SATs."

"Yeah, but you're a doctor. You're brilliant."

"I work at it." He winked.

He glanced at Ruth, who suddenly seemed distracted.

"Ruth?" he questioned.

"Where's your mother?" Ruth asked Gwen.

"Getting coffee with Maddie."

"Can you have her find me when she returns?"

"Why? Is something wrong?" Gwen's eyes widened.

"No, everything's fine. I'd like to go over your care instructions for when you go home."

"See, she's talking discharge." Spence patted Gwen's shoulder. "I need to speak with Dr. Carver for a minute."

Spence motioned Ruth out of the room. Once in the hallway and out of earshot, Spence turned to his friend. "What is it? Are her injuries more serious than you've let on?"

"No, that's not it." Ruth sighed, hugging her tablet to her chest. "The ER is swamped. I'm down two doctors and we're barely able to keep up. If there's a big emergency we'll have to send patients to Cedar River, which could potentially affect our reputation and maybe even our rating."

"It's about serving the people we can serve."

"I know, but the board is on my back to keep our numbers competitive."

"You can't control what's happened to me, or Dr. Danner's mysterious absence."

"I don't feel like I can control anything lately. Ah well, thanks for the shoulder."

"I'm feeling better. Do you want to reconsider me for the rotation?"

"Have you resolved who's after you?"

"No, but —"

"Oh, Spence." She placed a hand on his arm. "You're a dear, but the last thing I need is for your trouble to follow you here and put patients at risk. If you were thinking clearly you wouldn't have asked, can't you see that?"

"I was just trying to help."

"I know, and I appreciate it. But it would be best to keep your distance from the hospital until this settles down."

He nodded and she offered a kind smile. "Are you still staying at the resort?"

"Yes."

"Good, be safe."

Maddie and Allison approached them.

"Mrs. Taylor, I'd like to talk to you about how to care for your daughter once she's released." Ruth led Allison back into Gwen's room.

"How'd your talk go with Gwen?" Maddie asked.

"Good."

"You're not convincing me."

"Something she said is bothering me."

"What?"

"Why would the guy feel the need to hurt Gwen if his face was covered by the mask?"

"Where are you going with this?"

"Maybe she knew him, but isn't able to identify him. Perhaps one of her criminal friends who's dealing drugs. But why kill me?"

"He was afraid Gwen would break down and reveal his identity to you?"

"Scary thought. I should let Nate know she might not be safe." Spence pulled out his phone and spotted a text message from Danner.

Meet me @ Crescent Falls. Alone. Or people will die.

TEN

Maddie didn't like any of this—the mysterious text from the arrogant doctor, Spence's decision to meet him, or the police department's strategy to stick close and listen through the small radio device Spence kept in his pocket.

Spence was hopeful this would help the investigation, that Danner had critical information about the case.

"You're sure you're up to this?" Nate asked Spence.

"Yes."

Nate eyed Maddie in the rearview mirror for confirmation. She shrugged.

"Guys, it's not like we have much of a choice here, right?" Spence said.

"I could send Ryan up there dressed in your coat and hat."

"I appreciate your concern, Nate, but we need information in order to move this case along, and I doubt Danner is going to share it with the police, especially if he's into something criminal. I'm not sure you guys following me up there is a good idea, either."

"As opposed to you going out there on your own?" Nate snapped. "No, this is the best plan. You were right to contact us for backup."

Actually, it had been Maddie who demanded Spence get support from the police, even though he resisted. Danner wanted Spence to come alone, but Maddie wouldn't allow it.

She didn't trust Danner, nor was she sure Spence was in the best mental or physical condition to handle this on his own.

"Officer McBride and I will position ourselves to watch the interaction," Nate said. "If something feels off, we'll jump in to help."

"What could go wrong?" Spence said. "He wants to talk to me, that's all."

Ryan glanced over the front seat. "Then why did he mysteriously disappear without an explanation?"

"He's right, Spence," Maddie said. "We don't know what's really going on, or how Danner is involved."

Spence glanced across Maddie at the bodyguard on the other side of her. "Adam, keep her safe."

"I will, sir."

Spence didn't look convinced, concern creasing his features. She placed her hand over his, interlacing their fingers. He looked into her eyes.

"I'll be fine," she said. "Especially if I know you're focused, you're being careful and you're not taking any chances, okay?"

"Yes, ma'am."

They pulled up to the trailhead and the men grabbed their gear.

"It won't be dark for another three hours," Nate said. "Let's wrap this up before nightfall." He and Ryan started for the trail, but Spence turned to Maddie.

His expression of determination mixed with regret tore at her insides. She wrapped her arms around him and gave him a hug for encouragement. When she released him, he tipped her chin to look into his eyes.

"I… You…" she said, wanting to admit to Spence, as he had to her yesterday, that she felt a close connection to him, as well.

"I'll be fine," he said.

He brushed a quick kiss against her lips, turned and marched toward the trail. When Ryan raised an eyebrow,

Maddie crossed her arms over her chest. "Don't let anything happen to him," she said to her big brother.

Ryan offered a mock salute. He and Nate followed Spence, the three men disappearing from view.

Lord, please protect him.

She hadn't been able to confess her true feelings, and he was gone again, heading into a potentially dangerous situation.

"Let's get in the car," Adam said.

She climbed into the backseat and shut the door. What was the matter with her? What kind of coward would keep such blessed feelings to herself?

Someone who knew once you spoke the words, you couldn't take them back. You couldn't edit or revise them once they were out in the open. Yet deep down she worried that these feelings were born from this tumultuous situation, that perhaps this wasn't true love, this wasn't...

Oh, stop lying to yourself.

These feelings were real, and she feared the pain that would follow if she opened her heart completely to this complicated man.

Adam joined her in the car and shut the door. "They'll be okay."

She nodded, once again using the power of prayer to calm her fears.

Spence hadn't been completely honest with Nate, Ryan or Maddie, or he would have told them he wasn't functioning at his usual 120 percent. Today his energy level was more like 70 percent. Not good. Yet he'd just offered to get back on the rotation. Maybe Ruth was right about him not thinking clearly.

About a quarter of a mile from the falls, Nate and Ryan veered off and took another trail that would place them above the rendezvous point.

Spence's head had started aching a few minutes ago, and

his breathing felt more labored than usual. He reminded himself he couldn't be expected to hike at his peak performance, not after everything that had happened over the past few days, starting with the knock to his head that left him struggling with intermittent anxiety and confusion.

Yet he wasn't confused about his feelings for Maddie. Or was that part of the brain trauma? He knew such injuries could cause a patient's personality to change, that his way of thinking could have shifted, opening up his heart to the possibility of love and a life partner. If that was the case, could it shift back? Could he wake up one day and decide love was too dangerous to take a chance on?

Spence snapped his attention to the present. Maddie had asked him to stay focused and not take any chances. Well, he'd failed on the first count, as runaway thoughts about Maddie distracted him from the goal: find Danner and get information that could help put an end to the threat on his life, and her life.

As he approached the last switchback before he'd reach Crescent Falls, Spence sensed someone was watching him. He scanned the surrounding area, and his gaze landed briefly on Nate, who offered a thumbs-up from above. Spence ripped his gaze from his friend and continued on. Almost there.

The air was fresh and damp, the intensity of the falls pounding on rocks around the corner. He made the turn.

His breath caught at the sight of the powerful falls. He allowed himself to be enamored with the beauty of nature for a few seconds as he continued to the rocky shore that led to the massive body of water at the bottom of the falls.

He redirected his attention to his surroundings, doing a three-sixty scan of the area, looking for his colleague. He stopped himself from glancing at Nate in case Danner was watching from a hidden spot.

"Danner!" Spence called out, his voice echoing back at him.

As he gazed across the water, he noticed a splash of red on the rocks up ahead.

A body.

Instinct kicked in and Spence broke into a sprint. The spray from the falls showered him as he got closer to the victim. Someone—maybe Danner—was hurt and Spence could help. He reached the body and slowly turned it over.

Bill Danner.

Spence felt for a pulse. Rapid and shallow. Spence squinted in the direction of his police backup, and motioned for help.

Then he heard a click.

He turned back to Danner, who was pointing a gun at Spence's chest. "Who came with you?"

Spence raised his hands. "It's okay, they're here to help. I'm here to help. What's going on?"

Danner got to his feet and winced, clutching his side. His face went white.

"You're hurt. What happened?" Spence said.

"Like you don't know?"

Blood stained Danner's jacket.

"Bill, come on, let me help you."

Danner flicked the gun sideways.

"Put the gun down," Spence said.

"Move!" Danner threatened.

He was seriously injured and acting irrationally. Spence did as ordered, hoping to talk the guy into surrendering the gun.

Danner motioned Spence up a trail that led to a plateau beneath the falls. If not for the dangerous situation it would be a breathtaking spot, so close to the powerful falls as water cascaded from above to hit the small lake below.

Danner shoved at Spence from behind, and he almost went over, but fell to the ground instead.

"Why did you set me up?" Danner said.

Spence got to his feet. "What are you talking about?"

"Don't play innocent, Dr. Perfect. It had to be you."

"Bill, calm down, let's talk about this."

"Like you talked to the feds?"

"William Danner! Drop your weapon!" Nate called. He and Ryan were following them up the trail.

Danner didn't take his eyes off Spence. Heart pounding, Spence thought this was it, the guy was out of his mind and was going to shoot him in cold blood, in front of authorities.

"I'm not going to jail for something I didn't do!" Danner shouted, his voice competing with the pounding of the falls.

"Put down the gun and we'll figure this out," Spence pleaded.

"Last warning!" Nate called.

As Danner cast a nervous glance over his shoulder at Nate, Spence lunged for the gun.

They struggled, Danner weakened by whatever injury he'd sustained. Spence ripped the gun out of Danner's hand and he stumbled backward, falling into the water below.

Spence dropped the gun and ripped off his jacket, ready to jump in after him.

"No!" Nate suddenly blocked him. "Officer McBride, go!"

Ryan ripped off his backpack and jacket, shucked his boots and dived into the water.

"I didn't mean for him to fall," Spence said.

"I know." Nate called into his radio for a search-and-rescue team.

Ryan's head bobbed up above the waterline, then disappeared again as he searched for Bill Danner.

"He was injured before he went in," Spence said. "He's not going to be able to pull himself up."

"Calm down, buddy," Nate said. "Ryan's done rescue work like this before. Why was Danner threatening you with a gun?"

Spence shook his head. "He accused me of setting him up, said I talked to the feds. About what? What was he into?"

Ryan popped his head up above the surface. He had his arm around Danner's chest and was pulling him toward the shore. Nate and Spence rushed down the trail and helped lift him out of the water.

"Let's start resuscitation," Spence said.

They took turns giving Danner mouth-to-mouth and doing chest compressions. Spence finally found a consistent pulse. "Got it," he said. "How long until SAR gets here?"

"Twenty to thirty minutes," Ryan said.

"Let's keep him warm and monitor his pulse," Spence said.

He wasn't going to let him die. He couldn't let him die.

"Spence," Nate said.

Spence glanced at him.

"Good work."

"But—"

"I saw what happened. It wasn't your fault."

Maddie had hoped for quick and easy resolution to whatever drama Dr. Danner was involved in. But when SAR team members starting showing up at the trailhead her hopes were destroyed.

She flung open the car door.

"Maddie, wait—"

She shut the door on Adam's protest and rushed to the first SAR member she knew, fireman Sam Treadwell. "What's going on?"

"Got a call for an injured male by the falls."

"Who is it?"

"I don't know. Gotta go."

"Really?" she said to herself. "I'm going to slug my brother."

"Why are you upset with your brother?" Adam asked, now standing beside her.

"He should tell us who needs rescuing."

"Come back to the car and I'll find out."

She nodded and went back to the SUV. Adam stayed outside, speaking into his radio.

Anger seemed like the better option right now because if she believed it was Spence who'd been injured, that might ignite a ball of grief in her chest that would consume her.

Ryan obviously knew how she felt about Spence after the very public kiss they shared. Why hadn't he notified Adam who'd been hurt? Unless it was Spence?

That was it. Spence had been seriously hurt and Ryan needed to tell her in person.

Adam opened the car door and handed her the radio. "He wants to talk to you."

She snatched the radio. "Ryan, I'm going to—"

"Maddie, it's Spence."

Emotion clogged her throat.

"Maddie?" he said.

"I'm here. Tell me you're okay."

"I'm okay."

But there was something odd in his voice. "Why did you call SAR?" Then panic struck her. "Is Ryan…?"

"Your brother's okay, too. The SAR call was for Dr. Danner. We'll be down as soon as we can."

"Thanks. I'm—"

"Maddie, put Adam on," Nate ordered.

Handing the radio to her bodyguard, she closed her eyes and let relief wash over her. She hadn't realized how tense she was, how close to completely falling apart.

A fleeting thought touched her consciousness—if this raw fear was what it felt like when potentially losing the man you loved, could she embrace love again?

Although Nate tried to get Spence and Maddie to go back to the cabin on resort property, Spence refused. He said he was done hiding from his troubles, and he was going to wait at Cedar River Hospital for news on Dr. Danner's condition.

Maddie chose to stay with him for emotional support. She could tell something intense happened at the falls, even if he wasn't ready to share the details.

Nate arranged for Maddie and Spence to wait in the doctors' lounge, a less conspicuous spot. As Spence paced from the soda machine to the refrigerator across the room, Maddie tried to come up with the right words to calm him down.

She struggled to figure out what was causing the anxiety: guilt or frustration? Or a little of both? Whatever it was, it could affect his recovery and she could no longer sit by and watch him stress out.

Relying on humor, she stood and bumped into him as he paced across the room.

"Excuse me," she said.

He tried stepping around her, but she blocked him again, and again.

"Excuse me, excuse me," she said.

"Maddie."

"Spence?"

"Why are you pestering me?"

"Because you need to chill out, Doc. You're giving me whiplash. Now sit down and talk to me." She took his hand, surprised he didn't pull away, and led him to a small sofa. They sat, but she didn't release him. "Dr. Danner will be okay, right?"

"I'm not sure."

"You and Nate resuscitated him?"

"Yes, but he was hurt before he went in the water."

"Hurt, how?"

"He seemed to be in extreme pain, had a puncture wound and he was acting irrationally." He started to get up.

She squeezed his hand. "Please stay here with me."

He leaned back against the sofa. "I'm hoping something he said can help authorities figure this out."

"What did he say?"

"He accused me of setting him up. I have no idea what he was talking about."

The door opened and Nate joined them. "Anything on Danner?"

"Nothing yet," Spence said.

"We found Alex Moors. Someone stole his truck yesterday so he wasn't the one shooting at Maddie and Rocky."

"Has the shooter been treated for a gunshot wound at area hospitals?" Spence asked.

"Neither Cedar River nor Echo Mountain Hospital have treated a gunshot victim."

"So he's still out there," Spence said.

"Do you think he died of blood loss and is lying on the side of the road somewhere?" Maddie asked.

"That would be a relief," Spence muttered, then glanced at Maddie. "Sorry, that was inappropriate."

"You're frustrated. We get it," Maddie offered.

"Detective Vaughn is investigating Danner's bank records, phone records, the works. We need to figure out why he thinks you set him up. What happened tonight has given us another piece of the puzzle."

"And what's that?" Spence said.

"There's something going on, maybe criminal, and Danner thinks you're involved. That could be why someone wants you out of the way, because they also assume you're involved. I need you to think, Spence. Try to remember anything strange or out of the ordinary that happened to you in the last month or so."

Spence shook his head, obviously frustrated. "Just the threatening emails."

"Did you find out who sent them, Chief?" Maddie asked.

"Not yet. IP address was the coffee shop in town. I'd prefer you go back to the resort instead of hanging around the hospital."

"We will, after we get word about Danner," Spence said.

The door opened and a nurse poked her head inside the lounge. "Dr. Spencer? The patient is asking for you. He's…" She hesitated. "He may not make it. Internal injuries."

Spence went to the door and Maddie followed him. Nate and Adam stayed close as the nurse led them to the ER area where they were treating Dr. Danner. Maddie feared Spence would blame himself for Danner's death.

"I can't let all of you in," the nurse said.

"We'll be right outside," Nate said to Spence.

Maddie touched Spence's arm, wanting to offer support, but it was like he didn't even feel it, like he was numb.

The nurse opened the door. The doctor treating Dr. Danner looked up at Spence. "I'm sorry. He's gone."

Spence wasn't sure what frustrated him more, the death of a colleague or the possibility that the death was related to whoever was out to kill Spence.

The worst part was seeing people get seriously hurt or die as collateral damage. This was Spence's fault because of something he'd seen or heard or knew, and someone wanted him dead.

Someone who didn't care if others got in the way like Gwen, Rocky and now Bill Danner.

Everyone was quiet on the ride back to the resort, especially Maddie. He could only imagine what she was thinking, something along the lines of "how did I get myself into this mess?"

The situation was getting worse instead of better, and Spence felt even more helpless than when he'd first been attacked in the mountains.

"Do you think it has something to do with the hospital?" Maddie suddenly said.

"Why do you say that?" Spence asked.

"Dr. Danner accused you of setting him up, yet the only thing you have in common is your work, right?"

"True, we weren't exactly friends outside of the job."

"Then maybe that's where we need to start. Something that happened at work involving the two of you."

Nate glanced over his shoulder into the backseat. "Did a patient die or sue the hospital?"

"We haven't had a patient die in the ER since I've been here. As far as lawsuits, there haven't been any filed against me."

Nate nodded and turned back to look out the front window. Adam drove and continued to scan the mirrors.

"We'll figure it out," Maddie said, placing her hand over Spence's, which rested on his thigh.

"Am I dropping you off at your aunt's farm or the cottage?" Adam asked Maddie.

"Take me back to Spence's cottage. We've got work to do."

Nate glanced over his shoulder again. "Like what?"

"A little research, nothing dangerous."

"Research?" Spence said.

"I'd like to try a relaxation technique to help you remember things."

"I don't understand," Spence said.

"You've been under a lot of stress. When we're stressed out, we can't focus clearly on things that should have raised red flags but we've brushed them aside because of our stress."

"You're going to hypnotize him?" Nate said.

"No, nothing like that. Look, Spence has been in fight-or-flight mode for days. His body and mind can't drift into a relaxed state, so he's unable to access important memories because he's like a Ping-Pong ball, bouncing all over the place. If you can relax the body and quiet the mind, things come to you that you don't notice when your mind's active and anxious. Does that make sense?"

"It does, but I'm not sure anything could get me to relax right now," Spence said.

"It's worth a try. Worst-case scenario is you won't remember anything, but you'll feel safe and relaxed for a few minutes."

"That would be something different."

The thought of being conscious yet feeling relaxed for even a few minutes was a foreign, but welcome thought.

When they arrived at the resort cottage, Adam had them wait in the vehicle until he gave the all clear signal. A few minutes later, he waved them inside.

"I'm getting picked up at the resort," Nate said. "You two stay safe and I'll check in tomorrow."

"You got my message about Gwen possibly being in danger?" Spence said.

"Yes. Retired Chief Washburn has offered to keep watch, both at the hospital and when she's released."

"Good," Spence said.

As Maddie and Spence approached the cabin, he couldn't help but scan the surrounding area, looking for the next threat.

"You okay?" Maddie asked as they went inside and shut the door.

"Sure, just hungry I guess."

"I'll heat something up." Maddie pulled containers out of the fridge.

Once again, Spence had a quick flash of what a home must feel like, with a lovely woman humming her way through dinner preparation.

"Have them leave it at the front desk and I'll pick it up later." Adam's voice cut through his thoughts.

"More friends are dropping off food," Adam said. "I'm not sure how we're going to keep your specific location concealed unless we continue moving you."

"Like musical cabins," Maddie joked.

How did she do that? How was she able to joke and tease when so much tension surrounded them? That's right, she derived strength from God. He wondered if her God would forgive another sinner and embrace Spence.

Spence went to the kitchen to help Maddie.

"I've got this," she said. "Why don't you relax?"

He went into the living room and checked his phone for emails. "Here's something. The Tomlin family has relocated to Florida."

"The whole family?" Maddie said.

"Apparently. The oldest son got into college down there so the mother and daughter decided to move with him."

"Florida, the other end of the country. I think we can scratch them off the list."

"Which leaves Lucas and Roger."

"That's if we stick with the original list. I'm wondering if all this is directly connected to Dr. Danner somehow, that we should focus on him. Besides, I have a hard time seeing a kid like Lucas coming after you. He always seemed like a gentle boy to me."

"People aren't always what they seem."

Maddie pulled plates out of a cabinet and slid them onto the table. "You mean, like you?"

He eyed her. "What are you implying?"

"It's just that Dr. Dreamboat's smooth charm and good mood seemed like a cover for something else."

He shot her a crooked smile. "You see right through me, don't you, Maddie McBride?"

The cabin suddenly went dark.

"What—?" Spence said.

Something crashed through the window.

ELEVEN

Spence heard a pop followed by a hiss.

"It's a smoke bomb!" Adam said.

"We need to get out of here," Spence said.

"No, that's what he wants. Lock yourself in the bedroom with Maddie! I'll get that thing outta here and neutralize the assailant."

"Maddie?" Spence said.

She held up her smartphone that lit the way. Spence wrapped his arm around her and they went into the bedroom as ordered. If Adam wasn't able to neutralize the attacker, this could go bad very quickly.

And Spence would not allow anything to happen to Maddie.

That's when he realized she was trembling. The violence of the past few days must have finally caught up to her.

"Let's hide you in the bathroom," he said.

"But—"

He stopped her protest with a soft kiss. "I'm going to protect you this time, okay?"

"But I can help."

"You're helping by giving me piece of mind. Stay in the bathroom and lock the door. Call 9-1-1." He encouraged her inside and pulled the door closed.

Hand on the bed, he felt his way back to the desk and grabbed the sturdy chair. A solid crack to the assailant's head should do it. Hopefully Maddie had called for help and the police were on the way.

After a few minutes he feared that Adam had been assaulted outside, but Spence couldn't both protect Maddie and help Adam.

The silence inside and outside of the cabin made him edgy. What he wouldn't give for a peaceful evening alone with Maddie.

Instead, he hid in the bedroom. Waiting. He decided to use his intellect to outwit his attacker. Spence went to the window and scanned the property.

Someone kicked the bedroom door once, twice.

Spence opened the bedroom window.

The intruder kicked the door again.

Spence rushed across the room, standing beside the door. He gripped the chair, ready to strike.

Another slam.

The door flung open. Spence whacked the chair against the intruder's shoulders. The guy stumbled a few feet.

Spence hit him across the back of the head. The guy went down, giving Spence the opportunity to draw him away from Maddie.

Spence climbed out the window and took off toward the resort, then redirected himself, not wanting to bring trouble to innocent guests. Floodlights shone from the storage barn ahead, where SAR held their meetings. Spence aimed for the barn, knowing there'd be enough places to use as cover inside until help arrived.

He cast a quick glance over his shoulder and spotted a man stumbling after him. Good. Protect Maddie. That was all Spence cared about. Draw the danger away from her.

Spence reached the barn door, relieved that as a SAR team leader he knew the code to unlock it. He darted inside, left the lights off and found a hiding spot up on the loft.

With a calming breath, Spence texted Nate his location.

Surely Nate had returned to the scene. The wail of sirens outside confirmed his hope.

Spence stood flush against a storage locker, clutching a two-by-four in his hands. Deep breathing, he coached himself. He had to slow the adrenaline rush or it could make him clumsy.

The creek of wooden stairs echoed through the barn.

The attacker was closing in.

Bright lights suddenly flooded the barn.

"What are you doing in here?"

It sounded like Scott the security manager's voice. Spence peeked out and saw the masked attacker dive off the stairs and land on top of Scott. The men tumbled, fists flying. Spence climbed down the stairs and tried pulling the attacker off Scott. The attacker slammed Spence's back against a post and elbowed him in the ribs. Spence coughed and doubled over.

"This isn't over," the guy growled in Spence's ear and scrambled away.

"Scott?" Spence went to assess the security manager's injuries. "Hey, buddy, you okay?"

Scott cracked his eyes open. "Yeah. Who was that guy?"

"Same masked creep who came after me in the mountains." Spence examined Scott's face.

The barn door swung open. "Police!" Nate shouted.

Spence pointed. "That way!"

Nate and Red took off in search of the assailant.

"You should get ice on it as soon as possible," Spence said.

As he helped Scott sit up, a terrible thought struck him. What if the guy went back for Maddie?

"Nate? Maddie's still in the cabin!" he called out.

No one responded. Spence started to get up, but Scott stopped him. "Hang on."

Scott spotted his radio a few feet away and winced as he

reached for it. "Aiden, it's Scott. Maddie's still in the cabin. What's your twenty?"

They waited. No one responded.

Spence grew more anxious.

"I'm at the cabin," Aiden answered.

"Maddie is in the bathroom," Spence said.

Scott repeated her whereabouts into the radio.

"Roger that," Aiden said. "I found the bodyguard outside. He's injured but okay."

Spence sighed with relief.

Nate and Red rejoined them. "There's another door in back. He's gone but—" Nate interrupted himself, "Spence, you're bleeding."

Spence glanced at his hands, and then looked at Nate. "It's not my blood."

"Not mine, either," Scott said.

"How is this guy still functioning with an untreated bullet wound bleeding all over the place?" Nate said. "Come on, we need to get back to the cabin."

"Maddie!" someone called from the bedroom.

Maddie recognized Aiden's voice. She unlocked the bathroom door and glanced past him. "Where's Spence?"

"At the barn. He's okay. They're on their way back."

As Maddie went to the kitchen table, she noticed the windows had been opened to clear the cabin of residual smoke.

"You okay?" Aiden asked.

She sat down. "Sure, fantastic."

"I guess that was a dumb question." Aiden shifted onto the arm of the sofa.

"I don't mean to be snappy," she said. "But I don't know how much more of this I can take. Every time we think we're safe, something blows up in our faces, literally. Speaking of which, what happened to the smoke bomb?"

"The bodyguard took it outside and was clobbered by the assailant."

"Is he okay?"

"Yeah, but he'll probably have a headache. He's outside talking to Nate."

The front door opened and Nate entered with Spence, Red and Adam. Spence reached for her and she went into his arms. The automatic hug whenever Maddie and Spence were reunited felt so natural. Someday she hoped the hug would be motivated by happiness, not relief.

"Where did you go?" she asked him.

"Outside to draw the guy away from you."

"You get points for protecting Maddie," Nate said. "But I'm afraid this means we need to move you again."

Adam rubbed the back of his head.

"You need a trip to the ER?" Nate offered.

"Nah, just ice." He went to the freezer.

"Do you want me to talk to Quinn about using his fortress apartment?" Aiden offered.

"Who's Quinn?" Adam said.

"He owns the resort."

"No," Spence said. "I'd rather you stash me someplace where no one else will be in danger if he finds me again."

"What about the farmhouse?" Maddie asked Aiden. She hadn't let go of Spence's hand, and he didn't pull away.

"What, so I can put your aunt in danger?" Spence said. "No, that's not an option."

"But it gives me an idea," Nate said. He pulled out his phone and made a call.

As Nate conferred with someone on the phone, Maddie led Spence to sit with her at the kitchen table.

"Thank you," she said.

"For what?"

"Protecting me."

"Protecting you? I'm the reason you're in danger in the first place."

"Stop it. I was out for a walk in the mountains. You didn't ask me to join you, although that would be something to look forward to." She forced a smile. "You and me out for a pleasant walk, enjoying the crisp air and the stellar views of the Cascade Mountains. What do you think, interested?"

"How can you bounce back so quickly after having your life threatened?"

Maddie squeezed his hand. "It's this little thing I call faith. Besides, the image of us walking in the mountains gives me something to look forward to when this is over."

"I… I'd like that, too," Spence said softly.

"We're all set," Nate said, joining them. He glanced from Maddie to Spence. "Everyone okay?"

"That's one word for it," Aiden smirked.

He obviously heard them discuss their future romantic stroll.

"So, what's the plan, Chief?" Aiden asked.

"We'll use an Echo Mountain Rentals cabin as a safe house instead of keeping you here at the resort. It's off-season so the company has plenty of available properties. Since Cassie works there I'll have her make the arrangements. We'll play a little guessing game with the cars to make sure you're not followed to the safe house."

"I'm sorry about all this, Nate," Spence said.

"Not your fault, buddy."

"That's what I've been trying to tell him," Maddie said.

The next morning Maddie awakened fully clothed on a bed in the rental cabin. Someone had tucked a soft fleece blanket around her body.

Spence.

Maddie felt blessed that Echo Mountain Rentals had a three-bedroom cabin available to use as a safe house. Adam took turns with her brother keeping watch and sleeping, while she and Spence relaxed in separate rooms.

Not that Maddie slept much.

Events of the past few days filled her mind with anxiety as she relived the attacks. Only now did she fully appreciate how Spence must have been feeling since that first attack in the mountains: constantly on edge, afraid, nervous.

Somehow she'd been able to compartmentalize those feelings, at least until last night when she'd lost it and launched into an uncontrollable trembling fit after the smoke bomb crashed through the window. Her breakdown seemed so out of character considering she wasn't the type to fall apart. As a paramedic she'd seen gruesome things and had never lost her nerve.

Perhaps she was physically spent and emotionally exhausted from the accumulation of attacks since that first assault in the mountains.

She decided to pray for strength, a coping mechanism she'd perfected since childhood. She'd been so resentful when her parents left, but prayer had eased that pain, and eventually she'd learned to accept that which she could not change.

Finally, and only recently, her prayers had focused on forgiveness, in her mind the most direct way to grace. And thanks to finding grace, she'd grown to embrace all the feelings involved with learning to forgive. She suspected Spence could use some of that forgiveness, especially for himself.

"Lord, why do we have such trouble forgiving ourselves?" she whispered. She sat quietly with the question for a few moments, and then she got up to start her day.

The men had offered her the bedroom with the private bath, which she appreciated. Splashing water on her face, she wondered how Rocky was doing. She dried her face and gave him a call but it went into voice mail.

"Hey, it's Maddie checking in. Hope you're feeling better. Wish I could do more, but I've been pulled down a rabbit hole. You don't want to know. And I don't want another lecture. Anyway, text me and let me know you're okay, okay? Bye."

She glanced at her clothes. They weren't particularly

dirty, but she didn't relish wearing the same clothes two days in a row. Oh well, she'd have to think about that later.

She opened her bedroom door.

Spence looked up from a laptop on the kitchen table. "Good morning."

"Hi." She ambled toward him.

"Your cousin is picking up some fresh clothes and will drop them off at the police station for Nate to bring over."

She was impressed that he knew what she'd been thinking.

Ryan came out of the guest bathroom. "How are you doing, sis?"

"Hungry."

"We've got bagels and cream cheese in the fridge."

"And fresh fruit," Spence offered.

"Where's Adam?" she said.

"Getting some sleep." Ryan nodded toward a bedroom. "Coffee's on the warmer."

"Thanks." She went and poured herself a cup, then shifted onto a chair at the table. "What are you up to?" she asked Spence.

"Going through emails and reports, trying to figure out what Danner and I had in common."

"How's that going?"

"Nothing so far. Might help if I could get into his email accounts."

"We'll put somebody on it," Ryan said.

"You guys have got a lot on your plate," Spence said. "Trying to keep me safe, while investigating whatever is really going on, plus Danner's death. I'd like to do my part."

"Let's keep looking into your files," Maddie suggested. She made herself a bowl of fresh fruit and pulled a chair close to Spence so she could also see the screen.

Spence froze.

"Wait, is there sensitive information I shouldn't see?" she asked.

"No, it's just, you smell good."

She glanced at Ryan, but he hadn't heard the comment.

"Sorry," Spence said. "Another case of words slipping past the filter?"

"Actually, I thought it was nice."

The way he looked at her, she almost thought he wanted to kiss her. Probably not a good idea in front of her over-protective brother.

"So, back to your emails," she prompted.

Spence refocused on the screen.

As he scrolled through the emails, she spotted one titled Discrepancy?

"What's this?" she asked.

He opened it. "I ran into Heather Finnegan at the gro-cery store and she asked about a billing error. We don't get involved with billing so I forwarded it to Ruth, who sent it to Theresa." They both studied the screen. "Ruth got an an-swer from Theresa, who cc'd me on the result."

"What about this email from Danner?" Maddie pointed. "He sent this to all the doctors on staff." She read the email, in which he complained about medical supplies being short-changed, while profits soared. "Did you agree with him?"

"I never had a problem. I tended to delete a lot of emails I felt had been resolved or were a waste of time. Bill liked to stir things up so I may have deleted anything else with that subject line that came into my email box."

"Hmm. It would be helpful to see those deleted emails."

"But they're gone."

"Actually, my old boyfriend taught me a trick." She glanced at Ryan, who narrowed his eyes at her. "It's legal. I'm trying to access Spence's trash, not anyone else's."

"Be careful," Ryan said. "If you find something, we want to be able to use it in court." He redirected his gaze out the front window, looking for signs of trouble.

"We'll go into your settings to see if we can dig out the deleted emails," Maddie said.

"Old boyfriend?" Spence said.

"Old jerk boyfriend," Ryan clarified from across the room.

"Hey, you didn't always think he was a jerk," Maddie said, searching Spence's settings.

"How old?" Spence said.

"My age." She smiled.

"I meant how long ago did you break up?"

"About a year and a half ago. We dated for five years. I thought we'd get married." She wasn't sure why she said it, but for the first time it felt okay. Her chest didn't ache, not even a little.

"That serious, huh?" Spence said.

"Very serious. Waylan helped me through some rough times. He was a computer genius and got into a prestigious school in California, center of the tech world. After a few months he stopped returning my calls, my texts. He had an exciting new life with no room for the old small-town girlfriend."

"Idiot," Ryan muttered.

Maddie smiled at her brother's protectiveness.

"It's challenging when your career takes you in a different direction than the person you love," Spence said.

"Is that what happened with you?" she asked, not taking her eyes off the screen.

"What do you mean?"

"There was a rumor going around that you were married back in Portland."

"Never married, but I had a fiancée."

"And your career split you up?"

"Not exactly. It was shortly after Oliver Tomlin died in my ER and I felt that I needed a change."

She looked at him, incredulous. Life got tough and people ran away, including her father, her mother and Waylan. She couldn't believe Spence was one of them. "You abandoned your fiancée because of a work crisis?"

"It's more complicated than that."

"Sure it is," she said in a sarcastic tone.

Oh well, she couldn't expect his armor not to have a ding or two in it, could she? Better to know now, before she fell too hard and too deeply in love with him.

"I caught her with another man," he said.

Maddie's fingers froze on the keyboard. "Oh."

"It was probably my fault. I was so dedicated to my work I didn't have enough time to devote to my relationship."

Maddie looked straight at him. "Do you blame yourself for everything that happens?"

He shrugged.

"Well, stop. Bad things happen, and they often teach us new coping skills. So instead of blaming yourself for your fiancée's choices, feel the hurt of grief and move on."

"That's good advice."

"Just remember, your problems will always follow you, and God will always forgive you."

She went back to accessing his deleted emails. "I can only access trashed emails within the past thirty days, but since the first attack was this week, I'm thinking we should find something in here."

He placed a gentle hand on her shoulder. "Thank you."

"It's not that hard. I could teach you—"

"That's not what I meant."

She glanced at him. A slight smile tugged at the corner of his lips.

"All this shame I carry around, here," he whispered, closing his fist and pressing it against his heart. "Yet somehow you made it hurt less."

She couldn't breathe, couldn't think for a second, then snapped back to reality.

"It shouldn't hurt at all," she said. "You should let it go and surrender it to God. Let Him do the heavy lifting."

Spending time with Maddie made Spence realize what he'd been missing. They shared a kind of closeness he could honestly say he'd never experienced with another person. He'd loved Andrea, but she'd never understood his work, what made him so dedicated to helping patients. After their breakup, he suspected she'd been more enamored with the title of Doctor's Wife than with Spence himself.

Maddie McBride had never seemed impressed by Spence or anyone else, for that matter. She was a grounded, down-to-earth woman with a strong sense of spirituality. And being around her, feeling her trust in God, made him want to give it a try.

They spent the morning going through his files, ate lunch and then Maddie rested. Ryan and Adam took turns keeping watch, although Nate felt confident their location was secure. He said as much when he'd dropped off Maddie's clothes while she was napping.

Later that afternoon the bedroom door opened and Maddie marched out. She approached Spence, who was checking work email, trying to keep up with activity at the hospital.

"Something's bothering me." She sat down at the table and motioned to the laptop. He shifted it in front of her. "The financial discrepancy you forwarded to Ruth. What was the problem?"

"Heather said she was double-billed, both from Urgent Care and the hospital ER for the same treatments. Ruth said it was a computer glitch, that Theresa resolved the issue."

Maddie opened another email. "You didn't see this one because it went right into spam. This patient is emailing you with a question about drug charges."

Ryan wandered up behind them as Spence read the email.

"I remember," Spence said. "The patient was admitted

complaining of chest pains. We ran tests and determined he was having an anxiety attack. Stress can cause those symptoms."

"His wife is asking about two medications that showed up on her bill. Did you order these?"

"I don't remember." Spence glanced at Maddie. "I'm not sure I like where this is going."

"Well, there's either a glitch in the billing system at Echo Mountain Hospital, or—"

"Someone's committing fraud," Ryan offered.

Spence's phone vibrated and he glanced at it. "It's Dr. Carver."

Maddie nodded that he should take the call.

"Hi, Ruth, what's—?"

"Spence, I'm so sorry," she said.

He sat straight. "What's wrong?"

"It's the board—I tried talking them out of it but they're letting you go."

TWELVE

"I don't understand," he said, as the room seemed to tip sideways.

"They feel that considering your condition—"

"My condition?"

"Spence—"

"I was attacked. I deserve time to recover."

"They've lost confidence. Someone sent the board president a list of your odd behaviors recently, like running into a burning building at the resort, and trying to scale down a mountain screaming your brother's name."

"How could anyone know—"

"It doesn't matter. They won't risk keeping you on staff and using bad judgment, like you did with Gwen the other day."

"With Gwen? What are you talking about?"

"You were off rotation, Spence. You had no business prescribing a pain medication."

"Wait, I didn't—"

"You initialed the order. She had a reaction and her blood pressure dropped dangerously low."

"Ruth, you've got to believe me, I gave no such order."

"I have to go. The meeting is still in session. They've agreed to buy out your contract, but you're no longer welcome at Echo Mountain Hospital or Urgent Care. I am so sorry."

The call ended. As did his career, his life. His odd behavior these past few days, thanks to his head injury, could mean he'd never practice medicine again.

Never make things right.

"Spence?" Maddie said, touching his arm.

"The hospital is releasing me."

"That's insane," Ryan said. "They can't fire you for being injured."

Spence stood and went to the window, gazing across the vast expanse of green.

"Ryan's right," Maddie said. "They can't let you go."

"They just did."

Sudden clarity struck him head-on. He turned to Maddie. "It makes sense."

"Spence, no."

"What better way to shut me down than to question my mental state and ban me from the hospital?" he interrupted her. "They've repeatedly failed to kill me, so they dream up another way to destroy me. No one will believe anything I say if my mental ability is questioned. Ruth said I prescribed a pain medication for Gwen, but I didn't. So obviously I'm being set up."

"But you're a brilliant and kind doctor. And you're back to your old self," Maddie said with a lift of her chin.

The confidence and defiance reflecting in her eyes gave him strength in the midst of chaos. "You're right. I'm putting an end to this."

"Doc?" Ryan said.

"I'm going to the hospital to speak with the board."

"You're not supposed to leave this cabin," Ryan said.

"I've been hiding long enough, being shuffled around and putting people I care about in danger," he said glancing at Maddie. "I need to speak with Nate. I've got an idea that could turn this whole thing around and draw them out in the open."

"I'll call the chief." Ryan pulled out his phone.

Spence went to Maddie and searched her eyes. "Your belief in me has given me the strength to do what is necessary. It will be over soon, but this," he said as he took her hand, "will not."

She smiled and he pulled her against his chest.

"It's the chief," Ryan said, handing Spence the phone.

Maddie stepped back and studied Spence's expression.

"Hey, Nate," Spence said.

"Ryan just told me. I can't believe they're letting you go."

"It's a strategic move on their part. Maddie and I have a theory that someone at the hospital might be committing fraud, but that's not why I had Ryan call. I'm going to the hospital to appeal my termination."

"Spence, I'm sorry about the job, but I'm not sure that's wise. I mean, do you really think you can persuade them to reinstate you?"

"That's not the goal."

"Wait, you don't want your job back?"

"Right now I want to be free from this violence and feel safe again. I'll interrupt the board meeting, make an impassioned appeal, draw attention to myself and probably get kicked out of the building. Actually, Officer McBride shouldn't accompany me because I don't want to put him in an uncomfortable position."

"Your goal is to get arrested?"

"No, to draw out my enemy. While I'm shouting about being unjustly fired, I'll threaten the hospital. I'll make it clear that I've got evidence that could shut them down. I'll fire my bodyguard, flag a taxi and very publicly tell him to drive me to my cabin. You will be waiting, ready to arrest whoever comes after me for the supposed evidence. We'll get ahead of him, Nate. We'll finally put an end to this thing."

"You sure you want to do this? People tend to gossip and if word gets out you had a full-blown meltdown at the hospital it could ruin your reputation."

"Can't worry about that. This is our chance to outmaneuver these guys. Board meetings usually last four hours. It's already in session, so I've gotta act now."

"Okay, I'm in. It's three o'clock. Let's say you get to the hospital by four, speak to the board and then get a cab. That puts you at the cabin between five and five thirty. Detective Vaughn and I will be waiting inside. I've still got your spare key."

"Sounds good."

"I'll have Officer McBride take Maddie someplace safe."

"Actually, it would lend credibility to the situation if she's there to witness the fallout. We've been inseparable for days so it would look suspicious if I showed up without her."

"If this whole doctor thing doesn't work out, you could be a detective," he joked.

"I'll keep that in mind, thanks."

"Put Officer McBride back on the phone."

Spence handed the phone to Ryan, who received instructions from Nate.

"You thought all that up in the last five minutes?" Maddie said. "I'm impressed."

"Thanks. Do you want to go with me or would you prefer to sit this part out? It might get tense."

"Oh right, because things haven't been tense these past few days." She smiled.

"You've got a comeback for everything, don't you?"

"Well, make sure you come back to me after you lure that creep to your cabin."

"I promise." He brushed a soft kiss against her lips.

Spence stood before the hospital board and pleaded his case in the most intelligent and calm way possible. He truly was fighting for his job, but on a deeper level he was fighting for something even more important: the safety of those he cared about.

His friends, his Echo Mountain family and, most important, Maddie.

If pretending to lose his temper meant he'd seal the deal on his termination and be ostracized from the community, he'd accept the outcome.

He'd learned he was more than just a doctor.

Spence was a man who'd fallen in love with a remarkable woman, a man who'd grown curious about her faith, and considered the possibility of embracing the Lord.

But for the moment, he wasn't done speaking his truth to the board.

"I've grown to appreciate the tight-knit community here in Echo Mountain and would never do anything to jeopardize any of these fine people," he said.

"We understand your intentions are good," Barbara Tune said. "But you have to see it from our point of view. You're suffering from a head injury that has caused lapses in judgment personally, and professionally you prescribed a medication that harmed a patient."

"I challenge the fact that I prescribed that medication," he said.

"It has your initials," Barbara said.

"Someone must have forged them."

"Dr. Spencer," Vince Brunson, board president started, "Crying conspiracy does not help your case. If you're not of sound mind, you wouldn't know you're putting patients at risk. You'll have to trust us to do our job and weigh the facts."

"I'd like to know who brought you that information, personal information, about what's been going on the past few days."

"Do you deny these events happened?" Vince said.

"I do not. But there were extenuating circumstances."

"We know you were attacked and almost killed in the mountains, and we're truly sorry," Anna Estes said. "This isn't personal."

"Yet you're using personal experiences, traumatic experiences, as just cause to release me. I've been under a lot of pressure these past few days. I've been assaulted multiple times—"

"Yet you requested to get back on the rotation," Vince said.

"I didn't want to abandon the hospital."

"So you'd chance your enemies following you into the hospital, thereby putting patients at risk?" Vince leaned back in his chair. "What are you into, Dr. Spencer? I'm curious what you do in your off hours that led to this violence."

Heat rushed to Spence's cheeks. No, none of this was his fault and thanks to Maddie he finally felt that truth in his heart.

"Sir, I was lured into the mountains where I was assaulted. I've been threatened ever since, and I have no idea who's after me or why."

"Which is exactly why you should stay away from Echo Mountain Hospital."

"But to be fired? Is that really necessary?"

"The decision's been made," Vince said. "Dr. Carver shouldn't have let you in here. You're dismissed."

"I'm not done."

Vince glanced at Spence, and then motioned to Ruth. "Call security."

This was it. The drama was about to unfold.

"Sir," Spence said.

A few board members glanced down at their papers in uncomfortable silence. Board president Brunson narrowed his eyes at Spence and muttered, "Shoulda known you were too good to be true."

The door opened and a security officer entered the room.

"Escort Dr. Spencer out of the hospital," Vince said.

Ruth shot a helpless glance in Spence's direction.

The officer reached for Spence's arm.

"I know the way." Spence went to the door, stopped, and turned to the board. "You're making a mistake."

With a grip of Spence's arm, the officer pulled him out of the boardroom.

"This is ludicrous," Spence said as the guard escorted him to the exit. He spotted Maddie and Adam at the end of the hall near the doors.

"They have no right to dismiss me!" Spence shouted. "This isn't over!"

"Spence, calm down," Maddie said.

The guard marched him outside where people passed by glancing his way with interest. Spence yanked his arm free. "Enough!"

His friends stepped up beside him. The security guard waited near the door to make sure Spence didn't reenter the hospital.

"Hey, it'll be okay," Maddie said.

"Stay away from me. Everyone stay away."

"I'll get the car, sir," Adam said.

"Don't bother. I'm done with all of you, this hospital, this ridiculous town."

"Don't talk like that," Maddie said.

"They think they've got stuff on me to justify my release?" Spence said. "I've got even more on them." He motioned to a nearby cab, hired by Nate in advance.

"Dr. Spencer, let us help you," Adam said.

"What, you think I'm crazy, too? You won't after you see what I've got on these brainless bobbleheads." He yanked open the cab door and clearly gave his address to the driver before climbing into the backseat.

As the cab pulled away, Spence glanced back only once, in time to see Maddie's genuine frown.

Well played, he thought.

Now he hoped it was worth it and the attacker followed him home.

Adam dropped Maddie off at the Echo Mountain rental house where Ryan was waiting. Since Spence was under

Nate's protection, and Maddie under her brother's, the bodyguard was released from duty for the remainder of the afternoon and evening.

Maddie ached to go home to her apartment for a little alone time, maybe to soak in a hot bath or read book as a distraction from what was going on at Spence's cabin.

He put himself in the line of fire to finally end the threat against his life. Some might think it crazy, but Maddie felt Spence made a good call, an offensive decision to throw the perpetrator off his game and draw him out for a change.

Spence was taking control and it felt right.

So much had happened this week. The attack on Gwen, multiple attacks on Spence, and…Rocky. She decided to check in and sent him a text. Instead of responding to her text, he called her.

"Hey, I didn't mean to bother you, but I wanted to see how you're doing," she said.

"I'm good, ya know, healing."

"I'd like to bring something over like—"

"Aren't you on the run with Dr. Dreamboat?"

"I meant when this was over. I'm hoping it will be sooner than later."

"How can you be so sure?"

"Got a hunch," she said.

"Well, I appreciate the offer, but I'm good. Vivian stopped by on her break and brought soup and a casserole, and some kind of crazy tea."

"It's healing tea from Healthy Eats!" Vivian called from the background.

Thank You, Lord, Maddie said to herself. She was grateful that Rocky's heart hadn't been so broken by Maddie's rejection that he wouldn't find comfort in another woman's arms.

"I'm glad Vivian's there," Maddie said.

"She's bossy," Rocky said.

"You like bossy."

"Yeah, I guess. So I heard the doc was fired."

"How did you hear about that already?"

"Someone at the hospital told Vivian there was a big blowout. The doc had a complete meltdown."

"Hey, I called to talk about you, not Spence."

"I'm good. I've got everything I need, plus the boss has approved paid time off for my recovery since it happened on duty."

"That's great."

"Yeah."

Silence stretched between them. It was as if Rocky had something more to say, but couldn't with Vivian in the room.

"I'm sorry you got hurt by all this," Maddie said.

"Make sure you don't get hurt," he warned.

"I won't."

"Really? Even when he leaves town? Because we both know you're not going anywhere."

That stung, not only because Rocky brought up the possibility of abandonment, but also because it felt like he was judging her again for needing to stay in Echo Mountain. Had he been right? Was she still in town out of some warped hope that her loved ones would return?

"Maddie?"

"I'm glad you're okay, Rocky. Take care."

"I didn't mean to—"

"Talk to you later." She ended the call rather abruptly, but couldn't stop herself.

His comment stirred up all kinds of fear and pain she'd kept safely tucked away. Sure, he'd commented on her motivation for staying in town before, but hearing it again made her wonder if she'd been fooling herself all these years. She thought she'd moved on, that she'd processed the grief of abandonment, but perhaps it was still driving her every decision.

"How's Rocky?" Ryan asked.

"Better."

"Then why do you look serious?"

"It was something he said."

"What?"

She glanced at her brother. "You think we do what we do because Mom and Dad left?"

"Can you be more specific?"

"Like you becoming a cop to protect people, like you always tried to protect me because our parents weren't around?"

"Yeah, tried and failed."

"I can't help it if I'm a self-reliant woman."

"In answer to your question, yes, things like that have to affect you on some level. Although I probably became a cop to boss people around because my little sister never listened to me." He winked.

"So, our past experiences drive our decisions?"

"Sure, that's how life works I guess."

Her phone vibrated with a text from Spence.

Checking in. How r u?

She answered that she was okay and praying for his safety.

When this is over and we are safe, will you take me to church?

She smiled as warmth filled her chest.

Of course.

Gotta go. <3

She held the phone to her heart and said another prayer.

"You'd better watch it or you're going to break that thing," Ryan said.

"What, the phone?"

"Your heart."

"Very funny." She got up and went to the laptop. "I still can't believe they fired him."

"He's been acting kind of funky since the knock to the head," he said, glancing out the window.

"He's fine now."

"If you say so, Doc."

"I do say so, and I'd like to give Dr. Carver and the hospital board a piece of my mind on the subject."

Her phone vibrated with a call and she hoped it was Spence, but instead, an unrecognizable number popped up. "Huh."

"Huh, what?"

"I don't know who this is."

"Let me answer."

She handed the phone to her brother. "Hello…? Sure." He held the phone against this chest. "It's Dr. Carver. Be nice."

Maddie snatched the phone. "Dr. Carver?"

"Maddie, I'm worried about Spence. He's not answering his phone. It seems like you two are friends so I thought I'd call you."

"I'm sure he's okay."

"He was so agitated this afternoon. I've never seen him lose his temper like that."

"He felt he was being wrongly dismissed. And I agree. I've been with him since the first assault in the mountains and his condition has improved significantly. In another week or two he'll be one hundred percent."

"I know, I know. It wasn't up to me. I did my best to persuade the board to give him time to recover before they made their decision. But they had concerns, like prescribing inappropriate drugs."

"He never prescribed that drug for Gwen and he'll prove it, along with other things."

Ryan got in her face and shook his head, indicating she shouldn't allude to the fraud case.

"What other things?" Ruth said.

"False accusations," Maddie recovered.

"Well, I hope he does. He's a fine doctor and a good man. That's why I'm so worried about him. If only he'd respond to my messages."

"I'm sure he will when he can."

"I feel responsible, like I've let him down. Oh, Maddie, if he does anything foolish like hurt himself."

"Dr. Carver, really, don't worry about anything like that. He's fine. I promise."

"Okay, well if you do speak with him…" her voice trailed off.

"Dr. Carver?"

"Who's there…? No!" A crash echoed through the line.

"Dr. Carver!"

THIRTEEN

Maddie jumped to her feet. "Ryan, call for help."

"What's wrong?"

"It sounded like someone broke into Dr. Carver's house."

"Dispatch, this is Officer McBride," he spoke into his radio. "I've got a suspected breaking and entering at…" He trailed off as he glanced at Maddie. "Where does she live?"

Maddie gave him the address. She'd been called to the doctor's house when her husband fell off a ladder and needed transport to the hospital.

"There was an accident on Highway 2. It might take twenty minutes to get a unit there," Dispatch said.

"That's too long. We can make it in ten," Maddie said.

"What's this 'we' stuff?"

"Let's go." Maddie grabbed her brother's arm and pulled him toward the door.

"Chief ordered us to stay in the cabin."

"Someone's got to help her, Ryan."

"I'll call Adam to relieve me."

"There's no time for that. Come on, Ry. I'll stay in the car until you secure the scene." Maddie rushed outside.

Communicating via text messages with Maddie had given Spence a great sense of calm. But it was time to focus and get ready for the perpetrator he hoped was on the way. Spence should have thought of this plan sooner, luring the guy out of hiding so Spence and the police could be in control for a change. It could have saved his reputation for sure. But more importantly, it would have kept a lot of people out of danger, especially Maddie.

When the violence was over and the case solved, what would happen to Maddie and him then? Maddie was a lovely, smart and positive woman, someone he could see himself traveling with, spending a week hiking in the Canadian Rockies. Her grounded nature pulled him away from the edge of panic, but there was more to it than that. She had faith in him, which felt…good.

Nate gave Spence a signal and put his finger to his lips. He must have heard something outside. Spence and Detective Vaughn shared a glance, readying themselves.

They'd shared their plan with Spence when he got to the cabin. Spence would pretend to be having a temper flare-up, going through files and looking for supposed evidence against hospital board members and staff.

Nate and the detective would hide out and wait for the assailant to break in. Spence hoped his performance had been convincing and word had spread that about him wanting revenge on the hospital. Drawing the perpetrator into their trap was a solid plan, but if he didn't get the message, Spence might have torched his reputation for nothing.

Detective Vaughn motioned to the bedroom. As they intensely focused on sounds coming from that part of the cabin, the tension threatened to trigger a headache.

No, he would not be thrown off because of that first assault in the mountains and subsequent concussion. Nate stood on one side of the bedroom door and Detective Vaughn on the other side. Nate motioned for Spence to continue going through files and shouting words of frustration against his enemies.

"They'll never get away with his!" he shouted. "Firing me? What right did they have to fire me?" Spence threw a mug across the room, shattering it to pieces. "They won't ruin my career with their accusations!"

A squeak from the other room indicated the guy had opened the newly-installed bedroom window.

"They're all going down, starting with the ego-driven Vince Brunson, then Barbara and—"

"Nobody's going down, Doc."

Spence glanced up. At first he didn't recognize the man because he'd shaved his beard, and his hair was blond instead of dark brown. He must have altered his appearance to elude authorities, but there was no doubt in Spence's mind: this was the man who broke into his cabin.

"What are you doing here?" Spence said.

"Finishing what I started." He stood just inside the bedroom as if skittish to join Spence in the main living area. He couldn't know there were two police officers flanking the bedroom door, could he?

"Why are you trying to kill me?" Spence said.

"You're bad for business."

"What business?"

Nate stepped into the doorway and aimed his gun at the perp. "Drop the weapon."

The guy didn't move at first, then let the gun slip from his fingertips. It hit the ground with a clunk.

"Turn around, hands behind your head," Nate ordered.

Detective Vaughn stepped closer, gun drawn.

Spence didn't move, wasn't sure what to do. It was over, well not completely, but at least the direct physical threat had been neutralized.

"I said turn around," Nate repeated.

The guy slowly turned, putting his hands behind his head. Nate grabbed his wrists and secured them behind his back with cuffs.

"Get in here and sit down." Nate shoved him into a living room chair.

"Hey, Chief," Detective Vaughn said, holding the perp's gun in her hand. "It's Officer Carrington's gun."

"So you're the guy who assaulted my officer the other night? You're just racking up the charges. What's your name?"

"Tom Wick."

"Tom Wick, you're under arrest," Nate said, and read him his rights.

Spence stepped around the kitchen island and approached the man, who was in his twenties. "Wait, Wick as in Wicker?"

Tom snapped his gaze to Spence.

"What's a wicker?" Nate said.

"Wicker is the name of the guy who deals pills to kids like Gwen."

"Is that right, Wicker?" Nate said.

Clenching his jaw, the guy glanced beyond Nate at the door.

"So this was about drugs?" Spence asked Tom.

"Sure," he said, sarcastic.

"Let's lock him up, Chief," Vaughn said.

"Ya know, Mr. Wick, once we shut the cell door, it's over," Nate said. "But if you cooperate, tell us who else is involved, we could advocate for you."

Tom shot him a look of disbelief, and went back to staring at the door.

Spence stepped into Tom's sight line. "Why me?"

Tom looked away.

"What do you think, Detective Vaughn?" Nate said.

"He doesn't deserve any mercy, that's for sure," she said.

Yet Spence had learned from Maddie that everyone, even criminals, deserved mercy.

"I don't know. I think he wants to talk to us, don't you, Tom?" Nate pushed.

Tom glared at Nate. "Lawyer."

Nate held his gaze, probably trying to intimidate him into

changing his mind. Instead, Tom snapped his attention toward the windows and his eyes rounded with fear.

"No!" Tom jumped to his feet.

Nate shoved him back in the chair. "Where do you think you're going?"

"Fire!" Tom shouted.

Spence, Nate and the detective were so focused on Tom they didn't see the bright orange flames crawling up the windows.

"Bedroom!" Nate shouted.

He grabbed Tom by the arm and pulled him to his feet. They ran into the bedroom, but flames sprang up across those windows, as well.

"Grab blankets," Spence ordered. "We'll soak them with water and make a run for it."

"We're gonna burn!" Tom shouted.

Spence pulled blankets off his bed, and Detective Vaughn grabbed one from the sofa. Spence flipped on the kitchen sink and quickly soaked each blanket. He worked best in a crisis, which was what made him a good ER doc.

After he and Detective Vaughn doused the blankets, they each took one.

"It'll help get us out without being burned," Spence said, grabbing the fire extinguisher.

"When you get outside, hit the ground and roll," Spence said. "I'll be waiting with the fire extinguisher. Keep your eyes closed when I blast you with the CO2."

Nate and Spence shared a knowing look.

"See you out there," Spence said.

Gripping the knob with the edge of the wet blanket, Spence whipped open the door and sprinted through the flames. Once free and clear of the fire, he dropped the fire extinguisher, hit the ground and rolled, smothering any residual embers on his clothes.

He jumped up, grabbed the fire extinguisher and turned to assist the others. With a guttural cry, Detective Vaughn sprinted out of the cabin, tossed the blanket and hit the ground.

"Close your eyes!" Spence shouted, and got her with a few short bursts of CO2.

"I'm okay, I'm okay," she said, and jumped to her feet.

The sound of a car speeding away drew his attention. "Look!"

"I'll try and get a plate number!" She took off in foot pursuit.

Spence refocused on the cabin, anxious for Nate and Tom to get out of there. What was taking them so long? They should have been right behind Detective Vaughn.

Spence got as close as possible. "Nate!"

Did they find another way out? Then a horrible thought struck Spence: What if Tom assaulted Nate and the perp went out another way?

"Go, go, go!" Nate shouted.

The two men burst from the burning cabin, Nate shoving Tom from behind. They both hit the ground and Spence shot them with the CO2.

"I'm good," Nate said, standing.

Spence examined Tom. "You okay? Were you burned?"

Tom gasped for breath, eyes wide.

"He was having some kind of attack," Nate said. "I had a hard time getting him out of there."

Spence noted Tom's labored breathing. "Asthma?" Spence asked.

Tom nodded.

Spence searched Tom's pockets and found his inhaler, held it to his mouth and administered the medicine. "Try to relax. You're safe now."

Detective Vaughn raced up to them. "I called in a description of the assailant's car. Units will be on the lookout. Emergency fire and paramedics are on the way."

"They'll send the engine from Wallace County," Spence said. "It's closer."

Nate glanced at the fire consuming the cabin, then back at Spence. "Man, I'm sorry."

"Yeah," Spence said.

Grief settled across Spence's shoulders. He'd helped build the cabin with a local contractor. Even though he hadn't planned to stay in Echo Mountain forever, it was his home, a place where he felt safe, and at peace. The locals had embraced him in a way no one else ever had.

A flash of memory drifted across his thoughts: Maddie in the kitchen singing her heart out. He would have enjoyed cooking a meal for her in his cabin.

"Good thing you cleared out the trees around the cabin or this thing could've gotten outta hand," Nate said.

"Which is why I did it. Plus the humidity and moist ground will discourage the fire from jumping."

"So now the question is, who set the fire? You?" Nate said, hovering over Tom.

Tom shook his head, his breathing strained. "No, no fire. Only—" he gasped "—give the doc an overdose. Make it look like suicide."

"Why?" Spence said.

Tom shook his head.

"Don't shake your head," Nate said. "Answer him."

"He paid me…five thousand."

"You were going to kill a man for five thousand dollars," Nate said, his tone flat.

"And stay out of jail…for dealing drugs," Tom admitted.

"The guy who hired you to kill Dr. Spencer is linked to the drug activity?" Nate said.

Tom focused on his breathing and stared straight ahead, the flames reflecting in his eyes.

"Let's go." Nate pulled him to his feet.

"The paramedics should check him out, Nate," Spence said.

"He's fine." Nate tossed Vaughn the keys and she went to get the car, which they'd hidden from view.

"Nate," Spence said. "I can't let you take him in until he's officially checked out."

"This guy tried to kill you, what, five times, and you're worried about his condition?"

"Five times?" Tom said.

"Unless you can't count," Nate snapped.

"I stole the girl's phone and passed it to someone. I broke into his cabin twice. That's it."

Nate got in Tom's face. "You used her phone to lure Spence into the mountains, where you tried to kill him. That's how this all started."

Tom vehemently shook his head.

"And you attacked me in the hospital, hijacked the ambulance with me in back and tossed a smoke bomb into my cabin," Spence said.

"No, not me. I stole the phone and broke into your cabin twice—the first time to kidnap you, and tonight to drug you."

"Who hired you?" Spence said.

"I don't know."

Nate narrowed his eyes.

"I don't!" Tom protested. "Got instructions from text messages."

Sirens wailed as emergency vehicles motored down the main road to the cabin.

"We'll figure this out at the station," Nate said.

Maddie and Ryan pulled up outside Dr. Carver's house, set back on secluded property. Ryan turned off the engine and looked at her. "I mean it, Maddie. Stay in the car. Do not get out, do not come looking for me. And lock the doors."

"Okay, okay."

Ryan got out of the SUV and pointed through the window. She hit the lock button and mouthed "thank you."

She watched him climb the front porch to Dr. Carver's house and hesitate. That's when she realized the door was ajar. He withdrew his firearm, eased the door open and disappeared inside.

Maddie waited for what seemed like forever. She checked her watch. Only a few minutes had passed. Oh, how she wished the paramedics and police would arrive.

She grew anxious. What if Dr. Carver was injured and needed medical help? No, Ryan would surely text her.

Her anxiety made sense considering the call from Ruth, plus Spence's plan to set himself up as bait to draw out the bad guy. Maddie knew they had probably turned off their phones, but she felt the need to make a connection with him all the same. She called him but it went into voice mail.

"Hey, Spence. So I'm sitting outside Dr. Carver's house, kind of freaking out here because we think someone broke in, and I wanted to say, I'll be glad when all this is over. I know that challenging times help us appreciate the good times and all that, but, well, I wanted to say I'm looking forward to grabbing pizza with you, or going to Healthy Eats, if that's your thing. Anyway, I hope everything went well tonight."

A flash of movement caught her eye. It was Dr. Carver stumbling on the fringe of her property.

"Oh no." Maddie pocketed her phone and jumped out of the car.

As she jogged toward the doctor, she considered how upset Ryan would be with her right now. But she couldn't sit here and watch the woman wander off into the surrounding forest.

"Dr. Carver?" she called out.

She kept walking, heading toward the trees, wavering from side to side. As Dr. Carver passed by a shed, she stumbled and collapsed. Maddie rushed to her side.

"Dr. Carver? Ruth?"

Maddie took her pulse. It was solid at eighty beats per minute. She pulled her penlight off her keychain and checked her pupils. They were dilated. Had someone drugged her, as well? Maddie pulled out her phone to text Ryan.

A firm hand shoved a cloth over her mouth. She punched and kicked, but couldn't stop what she suspected was chloroform from shutting down her brain.

Her arms weakened and her legs lost their fight. Darkness consumed her as someone dragged her into the forest.

After Tom was treated at the scene, Nate, Detective Vaughn and Spence headed to the police station. Spence struggled to fill in the blanks as he watched Tom say something to Nate through the one-way glass. Probably asking for his lawyer again.

The door opened and Nate motioned to Spence. "He says he wants to talk to you."

Joining Nate and Detective Vaughn in the interrogation room, Spence sat across the table from Tom.

Tom finally looked up. "Thanks, ya know, for the inhaler."

"Of course."

"You didn't have to do that." Tapping nervous fingers on the table, Tom finally said, "It wasn't personal, Doc. All the stuff that happened to you."

"I need to know why it's happening," Spence said.

Tom shrugged.

"Tom," Spence started, "I appreciate that you don't want to incriminate yourself, but I need answers. Without them my life and the lives of people I care about continue to be in danger. Will you help me? Give Nate something we can use to figure out who's behind all this?"

Tom considered. "I guess I'll be busted for the drugs anyway."

"And attempted homicide of two police officers and Dr. Spencer," Nate added.

"I didn't know cops would be there. Like I said before, I

was hired to make the doc overdose." He glanced at Spence. "Sorry. I was desperate for the money."

"And I'm desperate to get my life back. I've lost my job, which means I can't treat people who need my help, like you when you had your asthma attack," Spence said. "Please, tell us something."

Tom studied his hands and nodded.

"You've asked for a lawyer," Nate said. "Are you now waiving that right?"

"Yeah."

"Then let's start at the beginning," Nate said. "When were you first contacted about kidnapping Dr. Spencer?"

"I got an anonymous text last week. Said they knew about my business, but wouldn't go to the police if I did a few things, like kidnap Dr. Spencer."

"Kidnap him and do what with him?" Nate pressed.

"Leave him at Wallace Falls."

"What were you going to do, hike up there with an unconscious man over your shoulder?"

"I was supposed to leave him behind the public bathrooms at the trailhead."

"You have no idea who wanted him and for what purpose?" Nate pressed.

"No."

"And tonight's assault?"

"They promised me five grand to make him overdose."

"On what?"

"I don't know. They gave me the drugs."

"You're telling me you've never seen who's behind this?" Nate said.

"No, we had a drop-off spot. Same place I got my drugs."

"Back up. The supplier of your prescription drugs is also the person who wants Spence dead?" Nate asked.

"I don't know for sure. I leave money in a locker at the bus station and pick up a bag with the pills. Yesterday they texted me and said to pick up drugs at the locker, not my usual stuff. Something in the blue bottle would make the doc go to sleep."

"And then you'd torch the house?"

Tom shook his head. "No one said anything about setting a fire."

"Where's your phone?" Nate said.

Tom nodded at his pocket. Nate dug it out and scrolled through the text messages. "Vaughn," he handed her the phone. "See if you can trace this one."

"Yes, sir." She took the phone and left the interrogation room.

"How long have you been dealing to kids?" Spence said.

"Not long. It started with adults."

"You know what the sentence is for dealing prescription drugs in Washington State?" Nate said. "Add that to the assault and attempted murder charges and—"

"It got away from me, I guess."

"Then get it back," Spence said. "Do something to help yourself here."

"If I can tell the feds you helped us solve the local crimes, that would go a long way to helping your cause," Nate added.

"It wouldn't surprise me if he worked at the hospital," Tom said.

"Why do you say that?" Spence asked.

"Because when my supplier sold me the drugs, I'd also get a list of names of patients who'd been released with prescriptions for painkillers. My supplier must have assumed they'd make good customers."

The door burst open and Detective Vaughn motioned Spence and Nate out of the interrogation room. Once in the hallway, Vaughn said, "There was a break-in. Ruth Carver was assaulted, and…" She trailed off and glanced at Spence before finishing. "Maddie McBride is missing."

FOURTEEN

Spence couldn't think past the knot twisting in his chest. Maddie was missing? How was that possible? She'd been safely stashed in the Echo Mountain Rentals cabin with her brother, and Spence knew Ryan wouldn't let her out of his sight.

After locking Tom in a cell, Nate drove Spence and Detective Vaughn to the Carvers' house.

"What were they doing there?" Spence asked.

"Apparently Ruth was on the phone with Maddie when someone broke into the house," Nate said.

"They should have called 9-1-1."

"They did, but a car accident on Highway 2 slowed response teams."

"And so Maddie and Ryan decided to help her," Spence said. "Which still doesn't explain how Maddie went missing."

"We'll know more after we talk to Officer McBride," Nate said.

"He shouldn't have left her alone," Spence said.

The car grew quiet. Of course casting blame didn't help matters, but desperation drove his words. He was desperate that nothing should happen to Maddie.

Because he cared about her. A lot.

When they pulled into Ruth's driveway, he spotted an

ambulance. Spence jumped out of the car almost before it came to a stop.

"Spence!" Nate called after him.

As Spence rushed toward the house, someone called his name. He turned toward the source and saw Ruth being tended to by a paramedic on a front lawn bench.

"Ruth, are you okay?" Spence said, approaching her.

"Hi, Dr. Spencer," the paramedic they fondly called Wiggy greeted him. "She won't let us take her to the hospital."

"I'm not seriously injured," Ruth said. "Just foggy."

Wiggy packed up his gear and went back to the ambulance.

"What happened?" Spence asked Ruth.

"I was on the phone and someone broke in." She glanced at him. "I called Maddie because I was so worried about you after the blowup with the board."

"Why call Maddie?"

"You weren't answering your phone. Then I heard someone in my house. I was terrified, and ran out the back door. But I must have tripped and hit my head because the next thing I know I'm on the ground with the paramedic standing over me. But before that, I thought I heard Maddie's voice."

"She was with you?" Spence said.

"She was checking my pulse, I think. Where is she?"

"Ruth! Ruth!" Cal shouted, frantically stumbling up to them. He reached out and pulled his wife into his arms.

"Oh, Cal. I was so scared."

"I know. It's okay." Cal glared at Spence. "This is your fault. Now they're after us, too."

"Cal, don't," Ruth said, breaking the hug. "I'm fine. But the house is a crime scene so we'd better get a room at the resort." She nodded at Spence. "When you see Maddie, thank her for calling 9-1-1."

Spence couldn't respond, fear constricting his vocal cords. He assumed no one had informed Ruth that Maddie had gone missing, and he didn't want to upset her further. Cal led Ruth away without saying another word to Spence.

As Spence climbed the porch steps, he heard voices arguing inside the house. Nate blocked him at the door. "This is a crime scene."

"Meaning what?"

"We need to keep it intact."

"I understand. Where's Ryan?"

"Easy, Spence. He took a nasty hit to the head. If you can keep your cool I'll let you in, but stay in the front hallway."

Spence nodded and Nate let him pass. As Spence entered the house, he saw Ryan sitting on the stairs being checked out by the other paramedic, Vivian.

"No lacerations, and your pupils look normal," Vivian said, analyzing the back of Ryan's scalp. "We could transport you to the hospital just to be sure."

"No thanks," Ryan said.

Vivian stood. "Keep the ice pack on your head. And if your symptoms get worse—vomiting, passing out, memory loss—get to the ER ASAP."

"Will do."

Vivian left and silence filled the hallway. Ryan finally looked at Nate. "I told her to stay in the car. Why didn't she stay in the car?" he said, his voice cracking.

"We'll find her," Nate said. "I've got Red checking with neighbors about any suspicious vehicles in the area. Detective Vaughn, after we're done here I want you to go assist."

"Yes, sir."

"Tell me what happened when you arrived at the house," Nate redirected to Ryan.

"I searched the entire first floor but couldn't find Dr. Carver. I went upstairs and somebody clobbered me."

"They found Ruth out by the shed, unconscious."

"What was she doing out there?" Ryan asked.

"She was trying to get away from the intruder, tripped and hit her head," Nate said.

"But she remembers Maddie taking her pulse," Spence offered.

"And now Maddie's missing because she was trying to help," Ryan said. "Why? Why would they take her?"

"To get at me," Spence said.

"Maybe to make an exchange." Nate glanced at Spence. "You for Maddie."

"But if she can identify her kidnapper, they'll never let her go," Ryan said.

"He's probably wearing a mask, like he did before in the mountains," Nate suggested.

"Don't you have that guy in custody?" Ryan said.

"He claims he wasn't the masked man, which means there are more perps involved in this," Nate said. "Keep your phone handy in case he calls you directly, Spence."

"That's the best-case scenario," Vaughn muttered.

Nate narrowed his eyes at her.

"Sorry, Chief," she said.

"So what now?" Spence said. "I can't wait around for the next horrible thing to happen. I need to do something to find Maddie, do more digging to figure out who is involved."

"The feds have been called to investigate the suspected fraud," Nate confirmed. "But if you want to help, do your research at the station. I need to stay here and process the scene."

"I'll take him back." Ryan stood and motioned Spence outside.

As they silently walked toward Ryan's dark SUV, Spence couldn't chastise the man. Spence suspected Ryan was doing plenty of that himself.

As they got inside the vehicle, Ryan released a deep sigh, leaned against the headrest and closed his eyes.

"Do you need me to drive?" Spence offered.

"It's not my head injury." He looked at Spence with bloodshot green eyes. "I never should have brought her with me."

Spence knew that feeling, the feeling of intense guilt that grabbed hold of you and squeezed until you thought you couldn't breathe. He'd felt that same guilt after his brother had died.

Yet Maddie had shown Spence how to let go.

"If you hadn't brought her with you, she would have been alone and vulnerable in the cabin," Spence offered.

"If anything happens to her…"

"We'll pray that it doesn't."

With a nod, Ryan started the vehicle.

Spence glanced out the passenger window surprised that even though he was being sucked into a maelstrom of utter panic about Maddie's safety, the word *pray* felt natural rolling off his tongue.

The woman had truly affected him in the deepest way, a way he'd never expected. She'd shown him what true forgiveness looked like and opened his heart to faith.

Dear Lord, please keep my Maddie safe.

He hoped it didn't seem selfish to pray for her safe return. He had no idea how to appropriately pray for anything or anyone. Then he remembered Maddie's words: *You don't have to think about prayer. You just do it.*

So he did. All the way to the police station.

The pounding in Maddie's head felt like someone was tapping at her skull with a blunt instrument. And it was starting to drive her nuts.

She opened her eyes and struggled to focus. Where was she again?

A soft glow pulsed from a gas lantern on a table across the room. The room was empty except for the table and lantern. She sat up, leaning against a wood wall. She was on the floor of a rustic cabin.

Darkness reflected back at her through the multipaned window. It was nighttime.

How did she end up here? The last thing she remembered was checking on Dr. Carver.

Something was shoved against her mouth.

She lost the ability to fight.

Then nothing.

Standing, she pressed her fingertips to her temples in the hopes of relieving the pain. But why was she here? What did the kidnapper want from her?

As she went to the window, she realized she wasn't wearing shoes, only socks. She felt for her phone but her jacket was missing, as well. Glancing across the cabin, she noted a blanket on the floor where she'd regained consciousness.

Awfully considerate for a killer.

She wondered how long she'd been here. Hours? Days? No, the drug wouldn't have incapacitated her for that long.

The light from the gas lamp flickered. From the looks of the wick, it would probably burn for only another few hours. Then complete and utter darkness would fill the cabin.

Flurries fell from the sky as the full moon illuminated the white ground and snow-covered trees. If only she could escape the sparse one-room cabin. Thanks to the moonlight she could see well enough to find a path and hike to safety, even though she didn't know where she was exactly. She figured getting out of the cabin and fighting the elements had to be a better choice than staying here and waiting for her captor to return.

A soft vibrating sound drifted across the cabin. She snapped her head around, trying to make sense of where it was coming from.

The blanket—it was coming from the blanket.

She scrambled across the room, thinking it was her phone, that somehow she'd managed to keep it.

Tossing the blanket aside, she spotted a phone but it wasn't hers. She picked it up and read a text.

You are safe. There is food under the table.

Could this get any stranger? She reached below the table and pulled out a soft-sided cooler. She unzipped the flap and peered inside: fresh fruit, cheese and raw vegetables.

So she'd been kidnapped by a health nut?

Hang on, if he'd texted her that meant...

She called 9-1-1.

"9-1-1 Emergency."

"This is Maddie McBride. I've been kidnapped. I need help."

"I'm sorry, ma'am, what did you say your name was?"

"Maddie McBride."

"Please stay on the line while I contact our chief."

"Okay."

"Can you tell us where you are?" the dispatcher asked.

"I have no idea." She scanned the surrounding area. "Somewhere in the Cascade Mountains. All I see are lots of trees."

"Maddie, it's Nate. Are you okay?"

"I've been better."

"He hasn't hurt you?"

"No, and he left me dinner. This whole thing is seriously creepy."

"Describe your surroundings."

"It's a one-room log cabin with multipaned windows overlooking the forest. There's a wood stove, but no wood."

"Stay on the line. We're going to trace your phone signal."

"Okay, sure." She grabbed the blanket off the floor and cloaked it around her shoulders.

"Maddie?" Spence said.

Her fingers tightened around the phone. "Spence, it's good to hear your voice."

"What happened? How were you kidnapped?"

"I was checking on Ruth and someone grabbed me from behind. Then I woke up in this strange cabin with a massive headache."

"He didn't take your phone?"

"He did, but he left me a different one. It's weird, like he's trying to take care of me, like he doesn't want to hurt me. But Spence," she confessed, "I'm kind of freaking out here."

"You're a ninja, remember? And the toughest person I know."

She half chuckled. "Yeah. But if something happens—"

"Don't, don't say it."

She squinted to see better out the window. "But Spence?"

"Yes, Maddie."

"Oh, this is stupid."

"Talk to me."

"I was going to say, well, even with all the threats and craziness this past week, I've enjoyed the time we've spent together. That's twisted, isn't it?"

He didn't answer right away.

"It's okay," she said. "You don't have to agree in order to make me feel better."

"Maddie, I would give anything to be able to switch places with you right now because," he admitted, "I love you."

She closed her eyes, and felt a tear warm her cheek. "I thought I was crazy, ya know, because I feel this way."

"Then we're both crazy," he said. "Hang on... Nate is trying to tell me something."

A few long seconds passed.

"What's going on?" Maddie said.

Spence didn't respond.

"Spence?"

"Nate can't track the phone."

"Then how can I tell you where I am?" she said, gazing out the window.

"Have faith, Maddie. You taught me that," Spence said.

A man in snow gear, including face mask, came out of the forest and was heading toward the cabin with a definite limp.

"It's him. He's back." She stepped away from the window.

"How do you know it's—?"

"He's limping. It's the guy Ryan shot. Okay, okay," she said, considering her next move. "He's wounded. This could be my chance to get away."

"Maddie—"

"I've got to focus." She shoved the phone into her pocket and her fingers touched metal keys. Her house and car keys. She slid the keys between her fingers and curled up with the blanket around her shoulders, pretending to be asleep.

A thumping sound echoed from the other side of the door. He was tapping snow off his boots.

The dead bolt clicked.

The door squeaked open.

"Still asleep?" a man said.

She didn't move, didn't breathe. A surge of determination gave her a new kind of strength thanks to Spence's words.

I love you.

"Time to eat something," the man said.

She didn't answer. If only he'd come close enough, she'd nail him with the keys.

Adrenaline pulsed through her body all the way to her fingertips.

"Maddie?" he whispered.

She remained still, curled up. Floorboards creaked as he approached.

Through cracked eyelids she saw him kneel by her side.

She swung her arm and nailed him in the face with the keys. Stunned, he stumbled back and she jumped to her feet, delivering a kick to his gut. He doubled over and she raced past him out of the cabin.

Pulling the phone out of her pocket, she said, "I don't see a car, or other cabins, or anything. We're in the middle of nowhere!"

She ignored the wet ground chilling her stocking feet and the panic spiking her blood pressure. She sprinted toward the forest where she'd find cover.

"What else do you see?" It was Nate's voice. "Lights below? A clearing, anything?"

"Nothing distinguishable. There's no obvious road, either."

"Where's the perpetrator?"

She cast a quick glance over her shoulder, but he wasn't behind her. "He must still be in the cabin."

"Run, Maddie, run!" It was her brother's voice.

She practically dived into the forest but couldn't find a clearly marked trail. Without the moonlight, her vision was limited.

"It's dark and I don't have shoes or a coat." She kept moving.

Finally out of breath, she dodged behind a boulder and collapsed. "What now?"

"Keep the line open," Nate said. "We're still working on tracking your location."

She started shivering, her body's natural response to the cold, and she struggled to focus on something else, something other than the chill in her bones. Not easy when the moisture from the snow was soaking through to her skin.

"Hang in there, Maddie," her brother said.

"I think we've got something," Nate offered.

As she focused on her breathing, reality permeated her thoughts. They'd never get to her in time. They didn't even know where she was. And if they didn't find her soon, she could succumb to hypothermia.

Nate, Ryan and Spence kept talking to her, but after a while their voices seemed to fade.

She felt herself drift, then felt nauseous, dizzy.

"Have faith," she whispered, repeating Spence's words. "Have faith," she repeated over and over again.

"That's right, have faith," a man said.

Spence?

She glanced up and saw his broad form standing over her. "Spence."

He extended his hand and she took it.

FIFTEEN

"Maddie!" Spence shouted at the speakerphone.

There was no response. He glanced at Nate and Ryan, who stood close by in the conference room.

"What happened? Where did she go?" Spence said.

"He found her." Ryan slammed his fist against the table and paced to the opposite side of the room. He spun around. "Why couldn't we track the phone?"

"He disabled the GPS," Nate said.

"Then why let her call us at all?" Ryan said.

"To show us he's in charge," Nate offered.

Spence couldn't take his eyes off the speakerphone. Waiting, *praying*, to hear Maddie's voice.

"That's right," a gravelly male voice whispered through the room. "Watch your step."

Spence jumped to his feet. "Let her go!"

Nate placed a hand on his shoulder. "He's messing with your head."

"Almost there," the man said.

"His voice," Nate said. "It sounds like he's trying to mask it by talking from back of his throat."

Ryan stood in the corner, eyes widening with fury. "Come on, give us something," he ground out.

"I've got dry socks in the cabin," the man whispered.

"S-s-s-ocks," she said.

Spence's legs gave way and he collapsed in a chair.

"And we'll have dinner."

"D-d-d-dinner."

"Yes, you and me."

Nausea rolled through Spence's gut. He'd never felt such helplessness or desperation in his life. At this point he'd do anything to ensure Maddie's safe release.

"That's it," the man said. "Let's get you comfortable."

Spence's eyes were glued to the speaker, yet a part of him feared what might happen next.

Seconds stretched into minutes.

Nothing.

Nate glanced at his phone. "9-1-1 just confirmed the call ended."

Ryan shoved a chair aside and stormed out of the room. Nate spoke to someone on the phone in low tones, and Spence glared at the speaker with such intensity he thought it might melt.

"I don't care if he's in a meeting, we need assistance ASAP. A witness has been kidnapped." Nate headed for the door. "Hang on. Spence, I'll be in my office working on getting help from the feds."

Spence nodded, but couldn't speak. He had no words.

Nate left the room and the utter silence started to erode Spence's hope.

His fault. It was his fault.

Spence had involved Maddie in this by accepting her help from the beginning. Why hadn't he tried harder to drive her away? Instead, he'd leaned on her, relied on her and now she was being terrorized by Spence's enemy.

"God, I'll do anything," he whispered, assuming God understood his meaning.

And he would. He'd sacrifice his own life if it meant saving hers.

Because he knew he could not live in a world without Maddie McBride.

His phone vibrated with a call—a blocked number.

"Hello," he answered.

"I don't want to hurt her," a throaty voice whispered.

Spence's heart dropped. "Then let her go."

He stood to get Nate.

"If you involve the police, I will kill her."

"What do you want?" Spence sat back down.

"You."

"I'll do whatever you ask."

"I know you will."

An hour later the energy in the police station was stifling. Spence had finally received instructions on where to meet the kidnapper and when—three hours in the mountains beyond Deception Pass. But Spence had no vehicle or hiking gear.

He had a bigger problem: he had to leave the station without creating suspicion. He didn't like keeping Nate out of the loop, but he wouldn't risk Maddie's life if the kidnapper figured out Spence had backup.

For all he knew, the kidnapper had a partner in the police station. At this point they weren't ruling anything out, and Spence didn't trust anyone to save Maddie's life.

But he had the power to do so. And he would.

Reaching out to Ruth seemed like the best strategy. She and Cal were at the resort taking it easy. He asked if he could stop by, hoping to borrow one of their cars.

Spence approached Nate's office doorway and waited for him to finish his call.

"Good, keep me posted." Nate hung up and glanced at Spence. "How are you holding up?"

"I need to distract myself. Thought I'd check on Ruth at the resort. Who knows, maybe she remembered something else that can help us."

"I'll have Adam take you. I assume you want to be kept in the loop about Maddie?"

"You know it."

Nate called Adam and asked him to return to the station. As Spence went to the exit, he passed Ryan, who didn't even look up. Of course not, Maddie's brother probably blamed Spence for her being kidnapped.

Spence surely did.

He went outside and pulled his jacket closed in front. Glancing up at the mountain range in the distance he shook his head. If it was this cold down here...

Fighting the image of Maddie suffering from hypothermia and being tended to by a killer, Spence tried thinking of something else, anything else. But her bright smile and emerald green eyes filled his thoughts. Gentle, caring green eyes.

"Please, God," he whispered.

A few minutes later Adam pulled up and motioned for him to get in.

Ruth looked exhausted, Spence thought as he entered her resort room. She motioned him to the dining table and he sat down.

"Is Cal here?" Spence said.

"Went to get me something from the snack bar."

"Probably just as well."

"He shouldn't have said that before, about it being your fault. He was upset."

"I know the feeling." He glanced at his friend. "I need a favor."

"Sure."

"I need to borrow a car."

She leaned back in her chair. "What's going on?"

"I'd rather not involve you further."

"Please, tell me what's happened."

"Someone kidnapped Maddie."

"Oh, Spence."

"The kidnapper wants to meet, alone. I haven't told police."

"You can't go by yourself. It's too dangerous."

"I have no choice. I have to save her, Ruth. I have to..." His voice trailed off.

"You love her," Ruth said.

Spence nodded.

Ruth grabbed her purse. "Cal drove us over in my car."

"Will he be upset with you for letting me use it?"

"I'll handle Cal." She pulled keys out of her purse.

When Spence reached for them she hesitated before letting go. "Please be careful."

"I will."

Since Adam was posted in the hallway, Spence slipped out of Ruth's room through the patio door and left the resort without being detected. He didn't feel all that great about leaving his bodyguard in the dark, but felt he had no choice.

Spence decided to stop at a store outside of town to pick up clothes and a warm jacket since his things were destroyed in the fire. He also purchased blankets, boots and fresh clothes for Maddie, along with a thermal blanket to treat exposure.

Second thoughts about excluding Nate taunted him, but he couldn't risk involving the police.

An hour later he made it to the trailhead and after a short hike, he spotted the small cabin in a clearing. Heart pounding, he crossed the property and stepped onto the stoop.

What if she was gone? What if the kidnapper had moved her, or worse, killed her?

Please, God.

With a deep breath, he opened the door and went inside. The first thing he saw was Maddie on the floor. He quickly scanned the room, but she was alone.

If the kidnapper left her alone without locking the door that meant...

"No, no, no," he muttered, rushing to her side. "Maddie, can you hear me?"

He checked her pulse—sixty beats per minute.

Thank God.

Pulling off his pack, he dug out the warming blanket. Her clothes weren't as wet as he'd expected, which was good. He wrapped her snugly in the blanket and kissed her forehead.

"She'll be okay."

Spence whipped around and saw Ruth's husband leaning against the doorframe.

"Cal?"

"You know I'd never hurt her," he said in his normal voice. "She's a lovely girl and that family has been through enough." Cal stepped inside and locked the cabin door. He clutched a gun in his hand.

"I don't understand," Spence said.

"It's simple. You're too perfect."

"Excuse me?" Spence held Maddie close, stroking her hair.

"We had to do something to destroy your reputation before you opened a Pandora's box."

"You? That was you in the mountains with the mask?"

"No, that was Anthony. Mr. Wick procured her phone and passed it to Anthony. He was supposed to ensure you had a fatal accident."

"But why?"

"Stop pretending. You'd discovered our side business. You kept asking Ruth about billing discrepancies."

Spence shook his head. "No, Cal—"

"You were building a fraud case against us. You insinuated as much at the hospital board meeting. Anthony failed to kill you in the mountains, but then you suffered brain trauma and we decided to capitalize on that instead of killing you. Almost convinced you to kill yourself trying to save your brother."

"You were the ambulance driver, the doctor who led me into the mountains?"

"The one plan that worked in our favor. I had to draw

you out of whatever resort cabin you were hiding in and knew you couldn't resist saving people from a fire. Anthony drugged you in the kitchen and dumped you outside. Once paramedics got you into the ambulance I knocked out the driver and drove off. If only you would have ended your life then and there."

"But why kill Dr. Danner?"

"He was going to mysteriously leave town and we couldn't have that. An investigation of his disappearance would have exposed our operation."

"Danner was a part of this?"

"He discovered what we were doing so we paid him off. But he grew a conscience, the fool. Then your girl went poking around in hospital files and found potentially damaging information. We set up Danner to take the fall. Anthony was supposed to deal with him. He beat Danner up pretty good, but Danner got away. You'd think I would have learned to do things myself." Cal shook his head.

"So this was about money?"

"Money, and the fact I wouldn't enjoy prison food."

Spence continued to stroke Maddie's soft hair. "And Ruth?"

"Ah, my beloved wife. She came up with the idea."

Spence couldn't believe what he was hearing. "Cal…"

"What?" he shouted. "Don't use that condescending tone on me, Dr. Perfect Spencer."

Silence stretched between them. Cal had the power, the control. Spence glanced at Maddie, unconscious in his arms. There was no way he'd trust Cal with Maddie in this defenseless condition.

"So what now?" Spence said.

"You take this." Cal placed a medication bottle on the floor and toed it with his boot. The bottle rolled to Spence. "It's an easy way to go. You were so despondent about Maddie that you killed yourself."

Spence glared at Cal. "You're going to kill her?"

"No, but she was missing and presumed dead so you lost all hope," Cal shrugged.

Spence stood. "Take her to the hospital and I'll do whatever you want, after I get proof that she's been admitted."

"Who do you think you are?" He aimed the gun at Spence's chest.

"Those are my terms," Spence said. He loved Maddie and had to fight for her…to the end.

Suddenly Maddie started seizing.

Spence turned and dropped to her side. "What did you give her?" he shouted at Cal.

"A mild sedative, hours ago."

Spence thought he saw Maddie wink.

Cal stepped closer.

Spence spun around and tackled Cal.

The low rumble of men's voices awakened Maddie, but something told her not to open her eyes. She shoved back her anxiety and listened intently.

She heard Spence's voice, and then another familiar voice. Cal Carver.

"Who do you think you are?"

"Those are my terms," Spence said.

She'd heard enough to know Cal was the kidnapper, and he was threatening their lives. She had to do something to distract Cal so Spence could get the upper hand.

Pretending to have a seizure seemed like the best option.

Spence knelt beside her. She hoped he saw her wink, then…

He spun around and charged Cal.

A gunshot rang out.

There was nowhere to go, no place to hide in the one-room cabin. The men crashed to the floor beside her.

Another shot rang out. She pinched her eyes shut.

Pounding vibrated through the cabin. "Police! Open the door!"

"He's got a gun!" she shouted.

The police pounded again.

Cal and Spence continued to roll and punch.

The gun slid across the cabin floor. Scrambling for the weapon, she grabbed it and jumped to her feet, wavering.

"Stop!" she shouted, but the men kept fighting.

Due to the effects of hypothermia and the quick movements of the men, she couldn't get a clear shot off.

Nate, Ryan and Red burst into the cabin. Her gun was still aimed at the two men swinging at each other.

Ryan and Red pulled them apart.

"Red, cuff Cal and get him outta here," Nate said.

"Yes, sir."

"Maddie," Nate said. "You can put the gun down."

She glanced at him through watery eyes.

Ryan nodded that it was okay. She lowered the weapon and Nate eased it out of her hand.

"Spence?" Nate said. "Whoa."

Maddie snapped her attention to Spence. Blood oozed down his jacket sleeve.

"No!" She stumbled across the cabin and collapsed beside him.

"You're okay," he said, blinking those soft blue eyes at her. "That's all that matters."

Then, with a slight smile on his face, he closed his eyes.

SIXTEEN

Someone was humming.

Spence didn't know the song, but it didn't matter. He recognized her voice, even when she hummed.

"Maddie," he said, his voice raw.

"Hello there, Dr. Sleepy."

He turned toward the sound of her voice.

She smiled, a full-blown, uninhibited smile that warmed his heart.

"You're okay," he said.

"I am. And you'll be okay, too."

"What… Was I shot?"

"In the shoulder. The bullet went right through you."

"The police…how did they find us?"

Nate stepped up beside her. "I had Red keep an eye on you after Adam took you to the resort. Red saw you leave and kept you under surveillance."

"I wanted to tell you."

"It's all good. I'm glad we got there in time."

"What took you so long?" Maddie asked.

"We found Ruth's car in the parking lot, but weren't sure which trail to follow. Your brother figured out how to track Spence."

"What about Ruth?" Spence said.

"Arrested, along with Cal, Anthony and even Theresa,"

Nate said. "Apparently her flirtatious demeanor was meant to determine what you knew about the fraud scheme."

"So this wasn't about a personal enemy out to get me?" Spence said.

"No, sir," Nate said. "You happened to ask the wrong questions and they thought you were figuring it out."

"Tell him about Lucas," Maddie said.

"Right, the local teen who ran away from military school has been back in town for weeks," Nate said. "Broke into his parents' house and stole money and food. He was picked up at Camp Lakemont hanging out with friends."

"I'm glad he's okay," Spence said.

"Needless to say, his parents aren't pressing charges," Nate said.

"Nor are they sending him away again," Maddie offered. "I heard they're going to try counseling instead."

"That's good news. How's Gwen?"

"Back home with her mom," Maddie said.

"I didn't order that drug," Spence defended.

"No, but someone made it look like you did," she said.

"My guess would be Ruth," Nate said. "She also treated Cal's gunshot wound, which is why he didn't show up at a hospital."

"I still can't believe she was involved. And I had no clue," Spence said.

"You were focused on more important things, like saving lives." Maddie squeezed his hand.

That's when he realized they'd been holding hands. The warmth of her skin drifted all the way up his arm and uncoiled the tension in his chest.

"The feds are building the fraud case," Nate said. "Still hard to believe how it all played out. We're glad you're okay." He nodded at Spence.

"I'm glad you put a tail on me."

"I guess I know you better than I thought. Let me know when you're up to giving an official statement."

"I can do it now." He shifted in bed.

Spence wanted Maddie to leave. He needed time to process what should happen next, and come up with a logical reason that they should end their relationship.

"The painkillers might impede your memory," Nate said.

"I'd like to give it a try."

He slipped his hand from Maddie's. Her eyes widened for a second, then she smiled. "I guess that's my cue to leave. I'll check in later." She leaned forward and kissed his forehead. "Love you," she whispered.

She left the room and he released a heavy sigh.

"When did you figure out it was Cal?" Nate said, pulling up a chair.

"Not until he showed up at the cabin. I got instructions where and when to meet him. I found Maddie unconscious and tended to her the best I could. Then Cal shows up spouting nonsense about me uncovering the fraud, about Danner finding out and them paying for his silence. I was stupefied. I mean, Ruth?"

"She'd do anything to keep the hospital in the black. Not that it excuses her behavior, but she put some of the money back into the hospital."

"She had to know she'd get caught."

"I guess she thought she was smarter than the rest of us. What was Cal's plan for you and Maddie?"

"I'd kill myself because I was so despondent about Maddie being kidnapped. But she pretended to have a seizure to distract him."

"That Maddie, she is certainly special," Nate said. "The way she cares about people."

"Yeah, she almost died because she cares about me."

"That's not your fault and you know it." Nate stood. "Get some rest. I'll check in tomorrow."

Spence nodded and closed his eyes.

No matter what anyone said, a familiar pit grew in Spence's stomach: guilt, shame and remorse. It *was* his fault that Maddie had been drugged and kidnapped.

Love you.

When she'd spoken the words, his heart cracked a little bit more because he knew he shouldn't act on his feelings for her. He couldn't rip her away from her Echo Mountain family. She belonged here, but Spence…?

With all of his possessions destroyed, his home burned to the ground and his job gone, he didn't feel like he belonged anywhere. And he certainly didn't have much to offer Maddie.

No, he had depended on her enough, and he'd even fallen in love with her. But if he truly loved her, he'd accept that she deserved someone better than him, someone without all the baggage he carried around like a fifty-pound weight.

He'd stay in town long enough to help with any loose ends of the case, and then he'd quietly leave without fanfare or attention. After being checked out by a doctor, he'd get cleared to practice medicine again and start someplace new, someplace where they didn't know about his tumultuous history.

Your problems will always follow you and God will always forgive you.

She was probably right, but he couldn't think about that now. He needed to do what was best for Maddie.

Maddie needs you, a voice whispered.

He disregarded the voice, because if he listened he didn't stand a chance of getting out of town with his heart intact.

The next day he convinced Nate to let him speak with Ruth, who was sitting in lockup. Spence needed closure, an explanation, something. How could such a remarkable woman get sucked down such a dark path?

"You sure?" Nate said, gripping the door to the city's two cells.

"Yes. Is Cal with her?"

"He's in the conference room being questioned by the feds."

"Good." Some part of him wanted to believe it had been Cal's idea, and his wife went along with the plan because she loved her husband.

Nate opened the door and Spence entered the lockup area. Ruth glanced up from her position sitting on the cot. She shook her head and buried her face in folded arms across her knees.

"Two minutes," Nate said, and left them alone.

"Ruth?" Spence said.

She glanced up with desperation in her eyes, yet oddly not remorse.

"Why?" he said.

"There's a lot of pressure running a hospital, Spence. You have no idea. The board expects financial results and patients expect quality care and…" She paused. "Things just happened."

"And hiring me?"

She cracked a sad smile. "That felt like the one good thing I did. I hired a doctor who cared more about patients than the bottom line. Then you discovered what was going on, and our perfect doctor became a liability."

"But I didn't."

"It seemed like you had with all your emails and questions about billing. Anyway, it doesn't matter. It's over." She sighed. "And ya know? I'm relieved."

"I had no idea you were under so much pressure. I wish you would have—"

"What? Asked you for help? Really? Get out of here, Spence. You're making it worse with your platitudes and compassion."

He struggled to process how this could have happened, how he had no clue his friend was cheating the system.

"Go on," she said. "Go be perfect somewhere else."

Spence left the cell area and spotted Maddie's brother, Ryan, waiting in the hallway.

"Chief wants me to take you to the farm," he said.

"Okay, thanks."

With no place to live since his cabin had been destroyed, Spence asked to stay at the resort, but the McBride clan had a better idea; they invited him to stay at Margaret's farmhouse.

Ryan took Spence to the superstore on the way so Spence could buy clothes and toiletries. Spence was starting all over again. He'd done it before, but it felt different this time. He felt…melancholy.

"You sure I'm not putting your aunt out?" he asked Ryan.

"Nah, she lives to serve. Kind of like Maddie." Ryan shot Spence a side-glance. "So…?"

"So, what?"

"You and Maddie? You're going to dump her, aren't you?"

"That's a little harsh."

"Then you're staying around to date her?" Ryan asked, hopeful.

"I'm going to let her get on with her life without me."

"Sorry, Doc, but that's a lame excuse."

A few seconds of silence passed between them.

"Look," Ryan started. "I know my sister can be stubborn and bossy but she's a great person."

"You don't have to convince me of that."

"Then what's the problem? She really cares about you, and I sense you feel the same way."

Spence glanced out the window. "She belongs here, in Echo Mountain with her family. I don't."

"Since when?"

"Since the fraud, the kidnapping, the random assaults. My reputation has been destroyed and I can't expect the people of Echo Mountain to get past that."

"Come on, you know how forgiving these folks are."

Spence closed his eyes, withdrawing into his thoughts. Was Ryan right? Was Spence making excuses because he was afraid of being hurt again?

When they arrived at the farmhouse, Spence actually thought Maddie might be waiting with her bright smile and wry sense of humor.

Instead, the house was quiet. Margaret led Spence to an upstairs bedroom and encouraged him to relax. She said sweets and coffee would be available whenever he came down.

He stretched out on the bed, careful not to jar his arm. The splint reminded him not to exert himself in order for the gunshot wound to heal.

He finally felt safe, although emptiness consumed him.

Hours later he awakened to the sound of muffled voices drifting through the floor. He washed up in the private bathroom and cracked open the door to the hallway. It sounded like a party was going on downstairs. He shut the door and pressed his forehead against it. How could he face people after everything that had happened, after he'd been manipulated by someone he trusted? They all probably lumped him into the mix with the Carvers and Dr. Danner.

As a criminal.

Glancing at his suitcase, he was tempted to escape down the back stairs. Instead, he opted to greet the visitors. When he reached the front entryway, he could hardly believe his eyes. The living room was packed with local residents enjoying refreshments and laughter.

"There's Dr. Spencer," Margaret said, clapping.

The group broke into applause. Spence froze, unsure what to do.

Margaret approached him. "They randomly started showing up. But if you're too tired to visit…?"

"No, it's okay." He strained to see if Maddie was among them.

Her auburn hair didn't stand out in the crowd.

"Dr. Spencer, good to see you on your feet." Board president, Vince Brunson, approached him and extended his hand.

"Mr. Brunson." They shook. "I need to apologize—"

"No," he interrupted Spence. "I'm the one who needs to apologize. I jumped to the wrong conclusion. Chief Walsh told me what was really going on. I'm sorry the board took our frustrations out on you. To that point, we had an emergency meeting this morning and would like to offer you your job back."

"What? Wait, but my head injury, my erratic behavior…"

"Some of which was orchestrated by Dr. Carver. Besides, I'd like to think I'd be brave enough to run into a burning building to save innocent people." He smiled. "When your shoulder heals and you feel ready to return to the rotation, get cleared by an MD and your job will be waiting."

"Hey, buddy," Nate said, joining them. He nodded at Vince as the board president went to greet SAR member Sam Treadwell.

"This feels like a dream," Spence said.

"I wasn't sure if you'd be up for company, but when folks in town get an idea in their heads, well, it's hard to talk them out of it."

That's when Spence noticed a Congratulations sign hanging across a window.

"What's that for?" he asked.

"They're congratulating you for exposing the fraud scheme and surviving the week of being stalked."

"I... I'm not sure what to say."

"Hopefully they won't demand a speech."

Adam the bodyguard approached them and Spence reached out to shake his hand. "Thanks for everything. I'm sorry I skipped out on you at the resort."

"Apology accepted but I wish you would have let me help."

"At the time I felt like I couldn't risk it. So, what's next for you?"

"Heading back to Seattle tomorrow. New client."

"Hopefully lower maintenance than Spence," Nate said with a chuckle.

The men chatted briefly about the case, and then Spence spent the next hour visiting with each and every person in the room. He was stunned by their overwhelming support. They were curious about the week's events, genuinely concerned about his injuries, and supportive of his future in town.

Filled with conflicting emotions, he turned to go upstairs for a break and found himself face-to-face with Roger Grimes.

The man whose daughter Spence suspected had been abused reached out to shake Spence's hand. Spence hesitated.

"Please, Doc," Roger said.

They shook hands.

"I know I was angry with you, said some harsh words and I'm sorry about that," Roger said. "Thanks to your suspicions we found out Megan's boyfriend has been hitting her."

"That's terrible, Roger. I'm so sorry."

Nate joined them.

"That kid is some kind of bully," Roger said.

"Turns out he was the one sending you the hate email, Spence," Nate offered.

"You were paying attention when I wasn't, Doc," Roger said. "I can't thank you enough."

"You're very welcome."

"Speech, speech, speech!" the group chanted.

As Spence glanced at the guests, he spotted Maddie step out from behind a few SAR members. She offered her sparkling smile as if encouraging him to speak from his heart.

The guests quieted and Spence cleared his throat. "Thanks for coming to see me today. It's been quite an interesting week."

They chuckled.

"All of this, your well wishes and congratulations, means more to me than you can possibly imagine. I want you to know, whatever happens next, that I will hold this memory close to my heart, always."

He noticed Maddie's smile fade.

Spence held up his cup of coffee. "To the amazing people of Echo Mountain."

They raised their cups and cheered. Ripping his gaze from Maddie's, he placed his cup on the front table and headed for the stairs, needing to decompress for a few minutes. The heady emotions from the past hour were tearing him up inside.

"Spence?" Nate said from the bottom of the stairs. "You okay?"

"Yeah, sure. I'll be back down in a few minutes."

And he would, after he finished packing.

Maddie could tell Spence was overwhelmed. She suspected he didn't have much experience with such a supportive network of people. She wondered if he purposely isolated himself from others in order to protect them from his perceived failures. She'd put it together earlier today that he'd been running ever since his brother died. His fiancée's betrayal confirmed his failure at love, and then his patient dying in the Portland ER probably chipped away at his confidence as a doctor. Although he acted as if he hadn't been affected, Maddie could tell it cut him to the core.

She stood at the bottom of the stairs, wanting to go up and talk to him. But what would she say? How could she convince him to open his heart and trust love again? Trust himself, and God?

If there was one thing she'd learned from being abandoned by loved ones, it was that she couldn't control anyone else's decisions. All she could control was her own.

She'd never forgive herself if she walked away without fighting for something she cared about deeply. Maybe she could help Spence believe it was okay to forgive himself and take a chance, plant some roots in town and accept support from people who cared about him.

As she climbed the stairs, her pulse sped up. *God, please help me find the right words.*

Once she reached his room, she placed her open palm on the closed door. Took a deep breath, and knocked. "Spence?"

"Come in."

Opening the door, she sucked in a quick breath. He was packing a suitcase. She knew a part of him didn't want to go, didn't want to run away again. Humor and faith had always helped her in the past, and that gave her an idea.

Quirking her mouth into a teasing smile she said, "Hoping to make a clean getaway, huh?"

"Just getting ready."

"For the great escape?"

He shrugged. "I guess we should talk."

"About what—world events, church news, or maybe the latest gossip in Cassie's blog? Come on, I'll help you pack." She grabbed a pair of socks and rolled them up.

Handing him the socks she said, "Don't forget your resentment."

He narrowed his eyes at her and took the socks.

She handed him another pair. "Or your shame," she said with a smile.

She tossed a pair of jeans at him. "Oh, and guilt, you wouldn't want to leave guilt behind. You simply couldn't survive without all that guilt."

"Okay, I get it."

A slight smile teased the corner of his lips.

"Look, I've learned I can't change anyone's mind, nor should I. I don't know what your journey is or what God has in store for you, but what I do know is that you've been your own worst enemy for a very long time, always beating yourself up. I think people get used to beating themselves up and it becomes routine. That's what happened to me when my parents left, and then the boyfriend left. So, Dr. Kyle Spencer, I will not try to force you to stay in Echo Mountain, but I will continue to pray that someday you'll be able to let go of all that pain so you can experience true joy because that is my wish for the people I love." With a ball of emotion rising in her throat, Maddie wrapped her arms around his waist. This hug would have to last her a lifetime.

She released him and went to the door.

"Wait," he said.

Her breath caught as she fought back tears.

"Vince Brunson offered me my job back," he said.

She slowly turned. "No kidding. Then why are you packing?"

"Habit?"

Hope flitted in her chest. "How about trying a new habit," she said, closing the distance between them.

"Like what?"

She slid her arms around his waist again. "Like…love."

"Sounds intriguing."

"And surrender."

"Uh…not sure—"

"Surrender all that guilt, shame and pain to God. Let Him carry your burden."

"Maddie McBride, you are—"

"What? Bossy? My cousin Cassie always tells me that."

"I was going to say amazing."

"Oh, I definitely like that better than bossy."

He tossed the jeans on the bed, missing the suitcase completely, and framed her face with his hands. "Maddie, I love you, but I may not stay in Echo Mountain forever. I will go where I'm most needed."

She smiled, realizing the comfort of home could be found anywhere with the man she loved.

"Hmm, a life of service," she said. "I like the sound of that."

And she kissed him.

* * * * *

Dear Reader:

Running away from problems can sometimes seem like the right thing to do, but it's not necessarily the best choice. Feeling both joy and pain is part of the human experience.

Dr. Kyle "Spence" Spencer has been running most of his life, ever since he lost his brother in a tragic accident when they were kids. He shoulders the full responsibility of his brother's death. Yet instead of processing his grief fully, he chooses to save as many lives as possible, and run when a situation gets too intense.

Maddie McBride has always cared so much for her family, and even hoped that her nurturing personality would keep her parents from splitting up and moving away, but it didn't. No matter how much you care about people, you can't control their choices. Maddie guards her heart, fearing a painful outcome of loving too fiercely.

Will Maddie's love for Spence and promise of God's forgiveness encourage Spence to stop running? And if he can't stop running, will she be able to let go of her pain and open her heart to God's healing?

Life isn't always easy or simple. Relationships are complicated thanks to all the baggage we carry with us from our experiences. I hope you are able to process your experiences with love and then let them go. Holding on to guilt, shame or resentment only impedes our path to grace.

Wishing you peace on your journey,
Hope White

COMING NEXT MONTH FROM
Love Inspired® Suspense

Available February 7, 2017

THE ONLY WITNESS
Callahan Confidential • by Laura Scott
Paige Olson's five-year-old daughter may have witnessed her father's murder, but she won't talk about it—and now a gunman's hunting them down. Homicide detective Miles Callahan will do anything to protect Paige and her little girl...even if it means breaking police protocol.

SHADOW OF SUSPICION • by Christy Barritt
Framed for kidnapping her neighbor's daughter, computer specialist Laney Ryan needs help to prove her innocence. But as she and police detective Mark James dig into the case, they become the targets of an unknown threat.

DESERT SECRETS • by Lisa Harris
Kidnapped and tormented into revealing the location of her brother—and the money he stole—Lexi Shannon's convinced she'll be killed...until pilot Colton Landry comes to her rescue. But after their plane's shot down as they attempt to escape, they're thrust into a deadly desert pursuit.

RESCUE AT CEDAR LAKE
True North Bodyguards • by Maggie K. Black
When Theresa Vaughan is attacked at a remote snowbound cottage by a masked man seeking a secret from her past, her only hope of survival is Alex Dean, the daring bodyguard whose heart she broke when she ended their engagement.

PERILOUS HOMECOMING • by Sarah Varland
As the sole witness to a murder, Kelsey Jackson finds herself in a killer's crosshairs. But with the help of her high school rival, Sawyer Hamilton, she's determined to catch the murderer before she becomes the next victim.

PRESUMED DEAD • by Angela Ruth Strong
Preston Tyler's supposed to be dead...so Holly Fontaine can't believe the former soldier just rescued her from a bomb planted in her cabin. And with a killer after her, the childhood sweetheart she believed was gone forever is the only man who can save her.

SPECIAL EXCERPT FROM

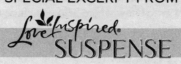

Love Inspired
SUSPENSE

*Paige Olson's five-year-old daughter may have
witnessed her father's murder, but she won't talk
about it—and now a gunman's hunting them down.
Homicide detective Miles Callahan will do anything
to protect Paige and her little girl...even if it means
breaking police protocol.*

Read on for a sneak preview of
THE ONLY WITNESS
*by **Laura Scott**, available February 2017
from Love Inspired Suspense!*

"I looked up the license plate of the black sedan from the restaurant," Miles said, his expression grim. "The sedan is registered to Sci-Tech."

"They sent gunmen after us?" Paige asked in a strained whisper.

"Yeah, that's what it looks like."

"They're after me because of my ex-husband, aren't they?"

"I think so, yes." Miles reached over and cradled her icy hands in his. "I'm sorry."

Paige gripped his hands tightly. "You have to find Travis before it's too late."

He didn't want to point out that it might already be too late. Whatever Abby had seen on the tablet had frightened her to the point she wouldn't speak. Had Travis told her to keep quiet? Or had she seen something horrible? He found himself hoping for the first option, but feared the latter.

"I'm not sure where to look for Travis," he admitted. "There's no way to know where he'd go to hide if he thought he was in danger."

"Did you give the police the list of names I gave you?" Paige asked. "I know they're only a few names, but…"

"I've been searching on their names, but I haven't found anything yet. At least we have another link to Sci-Tech. No wonder they were stonewalling me."

"I might be able to get inside the building," Paige offered.

"No." His knee-jerk reaction surprised him, and he tried to backpedal. "I mean, if they're the ones behind this, then it's not safe for you to go there. Besides, how would you get in?"

She lifted her uncertain gaze to his. "I know a couple of the security guards pretty well. If I waited until after-hours, when there's only one security guard manning the desk, I might be able to convince them to let me in."

"I know you want to help, but it's not worth the risk." He couldn't stand the idea of Paige walking into the equivalent of the lion's den. "You don't know for sure which security guard would be on duty. And besides, if anything happened—Abby would be lost without you."

She blinked, and he thought he saw the glint of tears. "Logically, I know you're right, but it's hard to sit back and do nothing, not even trying."

"I'll find a way to do something while keeping you and Abby safe." He couldn't stand the thought of her worrying about things she couldn't change. He'd protect her, no matter what.

Don't miss
THE ONLY WITNESS
by Laura Scott, available February 2017 wherever
Love Inspired® Suspense books and ebooks are sold.

www.LoveInspired.com